D1480690

FOLLOW THE RIVER

FOLLOW
THE RIVER

Paul Bennett

⤜⤐

Orchard Books

A division of Franklin Watts, Inc.

NEW YORK · LONDON

Follow the River is entirely a work of fiction. All names, characters,
and situations are imaginary, and any resemblance to persons living
or dead is unintended by the author and entirely coincidental.

Orchard Books   Orchard Books Great Britain
387 Park Avenue South   10 Golden Square
New York, New York 10016   London W1R 3AF England

Orchard Books Australia   Orchard Books Canada
14 Mars Road   20 Torbay Road
Lane Cove, New South Wales 2066   Markham, Ontario 23P 1G6

Orchard Books is a division of Franklin Watts, Inc.
Manufactured in the United States of America
Book design by Martha Rago

10   9   8   7   6   5   4   3   2   1

The text of this book is set in Fairfield.

Library of Congress Cataloging-in-Publication Data. Bennett, Paul L.
Follow the river. Summary: Growing up in a small Ohio town
in the 1930s, and acutely aware of his family's struggles to
make ends meet, "Lighthorse" Lee finds his fate firmly tied
to that of an intriguing rich girl and her family. [1. City and
town life—Fiction. 2. Depressions—1929—Fiction. 3. Ohio—
Fiction]   I. Title.   PZ7.B444Fo   1987   [Fic]   87-7911
ISBN 0-531-05714-3   ISBN 0-531-08314-4 (lib. bdg.)

To the memory
of my father, JOHN EMERSON BENNETT *(1875-1963),*
and my mother, MARY EVA GEHRING BENNETT *(1887-1971);*
and especially for
CHRISTINA JURIS BENNETT *and* LINDSAY JEANNE BENNETT.

But that same image, we ourselves see in all rivers and oceans. It is the image of the ungraspable phantom of life; and this is the key to it all.

—*Herman Melville*

Contents

State Park, Gnadenhutten, Ohio

HERE TRIUMPHED IN DEATH
NINETY CHRISTIAN INDIANS
March 8, 1782

PART ONE
1 9 3 0

≈ I ≈

The early morning sun painted afresh the small green house, one of two dozen clapboard houses bordering Walnut Street, the main business street of the town. From within the green house there came a din that momentarily drowned out the cooing of the turtle doves in the cemetery to the west of the town and the sighing of the presses of the tile factory to the east. A banging screen door announced the emergence of three of the six boys of the family—the three youngest, Hank, Hubert, and Harry.

Each of them carried a gleaming oyster bucket, and they spilled forth with those offhand, clownish movements that preserve personality when seven children and their parents cram a three bedroom house.

"I don't think they'll be ripe yet," Hank said.

"Neither do I," Hubert said.

"I could run ahead and see." Ten-year-old Harry moved in place with a coltish prance.

"Sure you could, you go ahead, Lighthorse." Hank spoke

with the authority of fourteen years' experience in life, and as one who had served his time as Run-and-See in the family. Having spoken he sat down and swung his oyster bucket between his knees, sat on the little jog where the badly cracked cement walk joined the ash walk in front of the house.

Hubert, two years Hank's junior, joined him, his blond head bent above his oyster bucket. Slowly and methodically he worked his tongue in and out, dropping spit toward the bucket but jerking the bucket away at the last instant.

Lighthorse tossed his bucket toward the two of them, saying, "Heads up." Then he set off at the cantering pace he could hold along green growing beans and peas and beets, around chickenhouses and barn-garages, across town, the quarter mile to the cemetery and the wild strawberry bed that flourished at its far end.

At a steady lope, conscious of the spring of his toes and the beat of his heart in his mouth, Lighthorse made the run. Running upwind into the mourn of the turtle doves, into the hard-warm texture of June sun on weathered white monuments and markers, he became aware of the give of the fine green grass of the graves, aware of the slight depression of some, and completely careless of what sleeping villager he trod upon. At last he stopped, his eyes sweeping the ground, storing the glow of sun on the wax green plants of the wild strawberries, hung with green berries and red—the red ones the size of the tip of his thumb.

"No berries, my eye!" he exclaimed as he fell to hands and knees to grab a sample handful. Then he retraced his run, past pig sties and chicken pens, alongside rhubarb and asparagus rows, moving in the fluid motion of great good news.

"Hey!" he called when he broke into Walnut Street

between the Ernst and Arkwright houses, two houses from his own. "Hey, Hank—Hube, come on!" He held up a berry and beckoned his brothers in one motion.

"You come here!" Hank called. He and Hubert got to their feet, but turned from him, walking quickly and shiftily toward town.

"What's up?" Lighthorse asked, running to overtake them. "Where you guys going?"

"Shut up," Hubert said, grabbing his arm and pulling him along.

"Yeah," Hank said, "you want Mom or Hessie to see us?"

"You guys aren't going uptown?"

"Of course we're not—we're going around this way to the berry patch." Hank began to run when he saw he was clear of the kitchen window. "Like hell!"

"But I tell you there's berries, lots of berries, and something might happen," Lighthorse said, when he caught up.

"Sure something might happen. The dead people might get hungry and eat 'em," Hubert said, as they slowed to a fast walk.

"Yeah," Hank said, "and then Hube and me wouldn't have to pick 'em, and that would be just too bad."

"But you promised Mom," Lighthorse argued.

"So what—you gotta promise her such things. Hell, she's a woman, ain't she," Hank said.

"Besides, we'll just shoot us a few snipes and then we can pick strawberries," Hubert said. "We'll keep our promise to her—" He acted as if he wanted to say *Mom* to correct Hank but he didn't.

"She'll be mad—plenty mad," Lighthorse said. "And if something happens to the berries . . ."

"Listen, you little bastard—" Hank didn't finish his threat. Lighthorse had slipped beyond reach, and continued

15

to pace them as they moved to the town square where they could find stubs of machine-made cigarettes.

Once they had their pockets bulging—shirt pockets were used to avoid crushing the stubs further—Hank's knowing nod called a conference. They stepped into the alley behind Dan Bird's confectionery and Hank said, "I guess we got time for a swim."

"I'd hope so," Hubert agreed. "You can't smoke out here in the street."

"Well you could out in the berry patch," Lighthorse said. His tone added: *if you have to.* "Besides, there are lots of berries and Mom wanted 'em."

"Will you shut up?" Hank said, offering his fist. "What-dya say?" he asked Hubert.

"Let's get a little swim." Hubert moved further into the shadow of the building, struck a match on the blue and yellow Mail Pouch Chewing Tobacco sign covering a rat hole, put an inch-long stub in his mouth, puffed rapidly, and said "Come on!"

Now they moved across town between apple trees and barns, following the alley to the swimming hole. And as they walked, Hank and Hubert talked through tight lips with cigarettes pinched awkwardly between thumb and finger, talked with the professional toughness of those who respect neither law nor man. At the outside, trying unsuccessfully to herd two stray sheep, ran Lighthorse. Where the alley stopped, they took a tortuous beaten path through the cornfield, and all three began to run.

"Come on, last in the water's a horse's ass!" Hank called, flipping his shirt into the towering nettles that shut off the grassy bank of the swimming hole from the cornfield. His pants were rolling away from his slender legs, and Hubert and Lighthorse hit him just as he leaped for the knotted rope dangling from the water maple. They fell, a tangle of threshing arms and legs.

Hubert's head bobbed above water first, then Hank came up and treaded to the left downstream, and Lighthorse arose some twenty feet beyond, throwing his head with a quick, practiced jerk to rid his hair of water.

"It sure feels great," Hank said, lolling back.

"Yep," Hubert agreed. "We needed a swim."

"Who the hell wants to pick berries anyway?" Hank asked.

"We promised Mom we would." Lighthorse slipped underwater as he spoke, knowing that swift flight permitted him to say what he had to say.

"I'll drown that little bastard." Hank treaded water, looking this way and that.

"If you could catch him, you mean," Hubert said.

Lighthorse surfaced some fifty feet downstream, arose like a gold river god borne aloft on unseen hands. And even as Hank moved toward him, he had seized new breath to disappear—only to appear again well past the middle of the stream.

"He's nothing but a damned dipper duck," Hank said, a note of envy in his voice. "He'd rather swim underwater than on top."

Again Hank and Hubert waited confidently for the towhead that matched their own, waited, sending their eyes in larger and larger sweeps. They were caught unawares when the head did appear, not across the river as they had expected but two feet behind them, to spray them with a mouthful of water before it disappeared again. This time Lighthorse appeared upstream, laughing, teasing them to catch him, and at the same time reminding them that they had promised to pick wild strawberries.

❧ 2 ❧

Later, gleaming tan in the sun, slicking the water off arms and thighs, they pulled on homemade chambray shirts and denim dungarees, garments faded white from repeated washing. The water still lingered along the fine gold lines of their eyebrows and the gold thatch of their heads, but gone was the taint of smoke, except for the bite on their tongues. And once more they moved off, swinging gleaming oyster buckets, moved around the eight-foot-high horsenettle-walled rooms—which were used as dressing rooms in the evenings, when everyone in town, men and women, boys and girls, swam together—to a footpath farther south, which led to Cherry Street, some two blocks nearer the cemetery and the wild strawberries.

On the way to the cemetery Hank and Hubert paused in old Peter Arkwright's garden long enough to snatch green onions, and then, with eyes watering, they approached Lighthorse to have him test their breath. The first and second time on each he shook his head. Not until they ate the onions to the bitter green tips—his sense of right made him force them on—did he admit that they were too oniony to smell of tobacco.

When they left the red brick walk of Cherry Street for the slag drive of the cemetery, Lighthorse realized they had come to the berry patch too late. Bobbing among the markers was the straw hat of Clem Philips, the aged caretaker, and sounding time for his bobbing hat came the gentle whirr of a well-oiled lawn mower. Before they ran forward with a cry of protest, Lighthorse saw that Clem Philips had completely mowed out the strawberry plants.

"Hey, Mr. Philips—hey!" Hank shouted.

"What's wrong? What's the trouble, boys?" Clem Philips stopped, let go his mower, and lifted his straw hat to mop a blue bandanna across his sun-reddened brow and over the top of a bald head edged with white hair.

"You cut up the berries—why'd you have to begin mowing here?" Hank asked.

"Yeah, Clem," Hubert said, "couldn't you have started over on the other side?"

"I could, but I didn't."

"But why didn't you? We was counting on those berries," Hank said.

"Mom told us to get 'em," Hubert said.

"Well now," Clem Philips said, "if I thought you really needed berries—you know how I feel about you boys." Then he turned from Hubert to Hank. "Why didn't you get yourselves out here a little earlier if you wanted those berries?"

"We was working—working at home," Hank said. "We had to help Mom and Hessie get underway with the washing. They're doing Doc Spears' and Horace Biggers' and the Owens' laundry." He turned to Hubert. Hubert nodded. He turned to Lighthorse, and for some reason Clem Philips turned his deep wrinkled eyes on Lighthorse too, as if Hubert had testified too quickly and was not reliable, as if Lighthorse were the final witness, the only witness.

"You look like you all been swimming to me," Clem Philips said.

"No," Lighthorse said, "you're wrong, Mr. Philips. Hank and Hube and I've been helping Mom and Hessie with the washing, like Hank said."

"Well, in that case"—Clem Philips ran his blunt, work-worn fingers through Lighthorse's hair—"why don't you three rascals run down the road to *my* berry patch and fill those oyster buckets. And see you don't tramp the plants," he added severely.

"Yes sir," Hank said. "Yes sir, we'll do that."

They started away, Hubert whistling, but Clem Philips called them back. "You know if I thought you three was lying to me I'd turn every last one of you across my knee. You wouldn't be lying, I reckon?" Again his dark eyes beneath the deep brows fired the question at Lighthorse.

"We'd never lie," Hank called as he moved quickly on again. "Not to you, Clem."

"No sir, Clem," Lighthorse agreed, turning away uneasily.

As they ran, Hank said to Lighthorse, "You fibbing bastard, you little fibbing bastard!"

"Lighthorse, you're the biggest liar of us all," Hubert said as they moved on to the jingle of buckets.

"I just—well, it was him or us—I mean all of us, Mom and Dad and all," Lighthorse said. "I didn't *want* to lie."

"Of course not, Lighthorse!" Hank said. "Of course not." He ran and tried to butt Lighthorse off into the bee-buzzing sweet clover lining the gravel road, but Lighthorse avoided him.

꩜ 3 ꩜

As soon as she saw the size of the choice strawberries Hank was pouring from the three oyster buckets into the eight used berry boxes lined up on the kitchen table, Mrs. Lee announced these were not wild strawberries, these berries came from someone's private patch. She heard Hubert boast they came from the Clem Philips' garden, picked with permission after he was fed a little story, and decreed the berries were to be paid for, pronto.

"There's only one thing I want to know," she went on. "Which one of you told Clem Philips the lie?" Anger and disappointment warped her mouth. As she spoke she untied her water-splashed apron, hung it across a chair back, and then pushed the hair away from her forehead, where perspiration stood in fine drops.

"Don't look at me," Hank said. He moved around the rinse tub away from his mother, but his eyes had fixed on Lighthorse.

Hubert too turned toward Lighthorse.

"Harry Clark Lee," Mrs. Lee said, "did you lie to that old man, and him with his heart trouble—why that's the next thing to lying to God Himself. Surely you didn't?"

"I just about had to." Lighthorse swallowed and turned away.

"He lied," Hank said. "Ask Hube."

"Yep, Lighthorse did it." Hubert exchanged a knowing glance with his brother. He too had seen Hessie waiting beside the pint fruit jars that bore each of their names, and he didn't want any of his life's savings to be used to pay for strawberries.

"Whose jar—his?" Hessie pointed at Lighthorse. "He ain't even got enough to pay for 'em. Eight quarts at ten cents is eighty cents." She handed the jar to her mother.

"Then he'll work it out." Mrs. Lee moved to the table where she laid out three nickels and began stacking pennies into piles of five each. "Anyone who'd lie to Clem Philips has enough metal in his heart not to feel a little work."

"I could tell you something," Lighthorse began as he watched his mother set his empty jar on the shelf beside Hank's and the other eight partially filled ones.

"You're not going to tell anybody anything," Hank whispered, wrenching his arm behind his back and giving it a quick twist.

"What's that?" Mrs. Lee asked.

"Aw nothing," Lighthorse shouted as Hank spun him free. "I just don't like you, all of you!" He swept the coins into his fist and moved to the door, but his mother caught him.

"Let go! Let go!"

"First you tell me where you're going."

"I'm going—up there—and pay Clem Philips."

"Well, all right." Mrs. Lee pulled him against her for an

22

instant and turned on Hank and Hubert. "Don't you two stand there acting smart. You probably put him up to it. That's it, get on outside, both of you."

Lighthorse looked up at his mother; he wanted to tell her she was right, but he wouldn't let himself. And as he looked he saw she knew. She went to the shelf and took down the pint jar marked "Mom" and from it took a quarter and two dimes and handed them to him without a word.

"I don't think Lighthorse lied," Hessie said, looking after Hank and Hubert. "That Hank probably made him."

"Mom, you don't need to give me your money." Lighthorse attempted to hand the silver back. "I can work it out."

"You just take it," she said, shoving him toward the door.

A minute later he called from the smokehouse shed: "I'll take the lawnmower, just in case he does let me work it out." He had already made up his mind: He would work it out, he had to work it out.

Mrs. Lee used her damp apron to wipe her forehead before she retied it and went back to the washing.

≥ 4 ≤

"Well, well," Clem Philips said when he saw Lighthorse, "it looks like I'm getting a little help. Need it too. This grass seems to grow faster than I walk." He stopped mowing, fanned himself with his straw hat, extended his long lower lip and blew upward. "That feels better!"

"I've got something to tell you, Mr. Philips," Lighthorse said, dropping his mower and going to stand directly in front of the old man.

"It's a stifling day, you don't need to tell me that." Clem Philips edged his mower into the shade.

"I'm not talking about weather." Lighthorse spoke as if reading a proclamation. "I came up here to tell you I lied to you. And Mom said I was to pay you whatever you would normally get for your berries. And I've got my own money and some of hers, but I'd like to pay only mine and work out all of hers—that's why I brought our lawnmower." He waved toward the mower as if he wasn't sure Clem Philips had seen it.

"Well now." Clem Philips smiled, got his handkerchief in front of his face and wiped his eyes and blew his nose. "Lighthorse," he said finally, "I believe you and I can do business—the way you put it, that is. Now how many berries did you get?" He sat down, and Lighthorse squatted before him, to face him eye to eye.

"About eight quarts—I guess that would come to about eighty cents."

"That's reasonable," Clem Philips said. "Of course you boys did the picking, now let's see." He caught up a sycamore twig and drew figures in the black ground. "That would be worth a penny and a half a quart."

"That's twelve cents from eighty, that only leaves sixty-eight," Lighthorse said quickly. He straightened and reached in his pocket. "I've got thirty-five cents of my own money and I'd sure like to work out the rest." He held out his handful of nickels and pennies.

"What's that pile of precious metal you got in your other hand?" Clem Philips asked.

"That's Mom's money—I'd sure like to work that out," Lighthorse said. "I can mow just about as good as a man. Dad says I'm as careful as anybody he knows."

"We don't need to be too careful mowing an acre and a half," Clem Philips said dryly. "And most of our audience aren't in a position to be critical."

"Well, I can mow fast too," Lighthorse said. "I'd sure like to work out the thirty-three cents—it's not really my money," he added.

"So you said." Clem Philips turned his face away, cleared his throat, and asked, "How much do you think you're worth an hour as a mower, Lighthorse?"

"Well Elmo and Everett get twenty cents an hour—of course, they're big."

"And they work by the day for Hans Baumholtz," Clem

25

Philips added soberly. "That truck farming's hard work, you know."

"Once in awhile Ed helps them unload a carload of lime, he gets fifteen cents an hour."

"He's a pretty big boy, even if he can't hold a steady job."

"He can too hold a steady job!" Lighthorse said. "If people'd only give him a chance—"

"But you will admit there are times when he couldn't hold a job steady," Clem Philips said.

"Ed's a good hard worker when he's all right," Lighthorse said. "Elmo says that. I heard Dad talking to Elmo about it, and Elmo says Ed'll straighten up. We'll just all give him a chance and he'll straighten up all right."

"Of course he will—if Elmo and your dad say that, he'll do it. Now how much—"

"We'll help him, we'll all help him—Dad, Mom, Elmo—"

"Of course you will. Now how much did you say Ed gets when he works?"

"He gets fifteen cents an hour unloading lime. Hank got to help once last summer—I think he got twelve cents an hour, or maybe ten."

"That unloading lime is hard work." Clem Philips shook his head slowly.

"Well," Lighthorse pinched his lips together and then smiled, "would you think I'd be worth a nickel an hour? If you did—it's about ten o'clock?"

Clem Philips tugged on the braided horsehide thong that looped from his suspenders, and caught the large gold watch in his hand. "Yep. Two minutes till."

"If you thought I was worth a nickel an hour and I didn't take any time out for lunch—six and one-half times five— I could just pay you off by four-thirty. Of course I'd owe you half a penny, but I guess I could give you one penny of Mom's money—I could always pay that back." Lighthorse held out a dime on a sweating palm and said, "You've got my money so you can change it."

"Now wait a minute," Clem Philips said, "wait a minute! If you pay me a penny and owe me only half a penny then I'll owe you half a penny. Now let me see—five cents for sixty minutes—tell you what: you work until four-thirty and six minutes more, and then nobody'll owe anybody anything."

"It's a deal," Lighthorse said, leaping to his feet.

"It's a deal," Clem Philips said, holding out his hand before getting to his feet. "Now you get your mower and line up—that's it."

≫ 5 ≪

For more than an hour they mowed steadily; they had worked their way to a cluster of trees when Clem Philips stopped before the largest—a giant honey locust—and asked: "Did you know there's a legend connected with this old tree? Come here. Put your hand in there."

Lighthorse ran his hand into a hole the size of a coat sleeve; the hole was smooth and damp and seemed bored right through the tree, but terminated a full arm's length inside.

"Tell me what you feel way at the back."

"It feels hard and cold—maybe a piece of metal." Lighthorse was digging his fingernails against the solid knobbed object.

"Nope. Guess again. Remember there were plenty of Indians hereabouts—Delawares and Mohicans. In fact, there was a big Indian massacre right here in Gnadenhutten back in 1782—white people deceived and murdered a whole passel of Christian Indians, you know."

"It—could it be a tomahawk?"

"Yep, a real tomahawk. Legend says this tree was just a sapling when the Moravian missionaries David Zeisberger and John Heckewelder came here in 1772 attempting to Christianize the Delawares." Clem Philips settled in the shade of the great honey locust, and Lighthorse dropped down at his feet and listened to the even rolling voice. "They weren't having much luck, as the story goes, when one of the old chiefs, Fishing Graybird, said he thought all his people needed was a sign, a permanent sign they should put away their weapons and live in peace. He told that to Zeisberger one Saturday night, and Zeisberger said he'd ask the Lord about it. He asked the Lord, pleaded with him from about seven o'clock Saturday night until time for services Sunday morning, and when they came out of their Sunday service they found that tomahawk stuck in that locust sapling, stuck tighter than teeth in sorghum taffy. This locust tree and that permanently buried tomahawk was the Lord's calling for peace. Yessiree, and after that everything was slick as sled runners for the missionaries. The Indians all threw their weapons away and became teetotaling Christians. They lived that way for some time; in fact, they were living that way in March, 1782, when a band of Pennsylvania militia moved in on them and massacred the whole kaboodle, men, women, and children—ninety-three in all."

"I knew about the killing," Lighthorse said with a shiver, "but not the tomahawk. That's better than the stories Dad tells about Dan Boone and Davy Crockett."

"Your dad tells some good stories. Even when he's teaching that Sunday school class of his, he tells some pretty good stories. And that's hard for a railroad trackman to do in church, believe me. Of course, your dad's no ordinary tie-tamping Gandy Dancer."

"Tie-tamping Gandy Dancer—he'd like that." Lighthorse laughed, then said, "I sure wish this tomahawk story was just happening now, instead of being done with."

"Why so?"

"Oh, I'd just like to see such a thing happen. Today everything seems to have already happened and we can only talk about it. Know what I mean?"

"Yep, I know what you mean. That's always the way life is. When you're close up, everything's already happened." Clem Philips fingered his chin. "Of course some few things are being done today—and a few things are waiting to be done."

"Like what?"

"Well now," Clem Philips laughed, "things like three boys going swimming and then coming here and telling me a whopping big lie, especially when I could feel the wetness of *your* head."

"You knew I had lied—even before I came back?"

"Well, I had a pretty good idea, maybe as good an idea as I'd have had if I saw you climb out of the river."

"I'm sure glad I came back though."

"It's costing you hard cash and harder labor," Clem Philips said. He mopped his steaming face and ran the wadded bandanna back and forth, across the pulsing veins that threaded through his scanty rim of hair.

"I've sure made up my mind on one thing," Lighthorse said. "No more lies for me ever. And," he added thoughtfully, "if I do tell one, I'm going to make it right just as soon as I can."

"That sounds reasonable to me." Clem Philips grinned down on the face candled by blue eyes. "By the way," he went on, "there was one young Indian woman the Pennsylvania militia didn't kill, couldn't touch, Lighthorse. Since we've been man-to-man about this lying, there's no reason we can't be the same about her story." Clem Philips cleared his throat. "There was this beautiful Indian maid whose parents were Delawares, and she made the mistake of falling for this young buck she met off on a blackberrying party. He was a Mohican. And of course her parents were against him. And the public—they were mostly Delawares—they were dead set against him, and a gang of them told this young buck to leave *Gnadenhutten*—cabins of grace—while he still had his scalp. And he did."

"He left by himself?"

"Oh, his girl wanted to run after him, even though he was an outcast. You probably don't know yet just how it is with women that way, Lighthorse, but when they like a man, they don't much care about what the public thinks." Clem Philips toyed with a heavy piece of sycamore bark, held it out to Lighthorse.

Lighthorse took the bark, noticed it unrolled like a scroll.

"Well," Clem Philips' voice went on, "things just churned on that way all summer, her moping and getting prettier and combing out her long black hair till sparks from it scorched the seed pods right under this very honey locust tree, and her trying to make some arrangement to get to her lover, who was said to be camping out solitary on the ridge over back of that bluff hill you can see in the blue distance. Things had come to such a pass she was ready to run away on her own to find her boyfriend, when her poppa relented. He told his daughter to get ready for her lover and to wait for him. I'll skip the details except to say she was so eager to see her boyfriend she didn't dress in anything but her long black hair. And her poppa arranged for her to be alone in their cabin, the nearest one to the Cooper Shop—over there right behind where that Indiana-limestone monument now stands. It was a bright moonlight night and she heard a couple bird calls and then a step outside the cabin door, and there was a man in the room—*but it wasn't her man.* Now she was a mighty agile girl and the best runner in the whole camp, so she got out of that cabin about as fast as a ground squirrel gets out of a skunk's den, and she made right for the river."

Lighthorse found the scroll in his hand pointing.

"Of course, this man—he had already paid her pa a jug of whiskey—took right after her, running down the river bank. The river happened to be in full flood, so naturally she couldn't dive in. But she did! And fool like, almost as if he'd drunk part of the jug before the bargaining began, her buyer dived in after her. Naturally he was a powerful swimmer and she was just a little Indian girl. Well, there's no need prolonging the story. She got her hands on him and drowned him the way you'd drown a rat in a sack. And then she climbed out on shore—or started to climb out by getting hold of a willow limb, but her pa came running and calling her names and demanding to know what she was going to do with herself. His daughter just kind of looked at him to make sure he could hear what he was shouting, and then she said, 'Well, Pop, old lout, if that's the way you feel, I'll wait for my lover here.' She turned and dove right back in that flooded river, a perfect dive that hung a little splash of water and two graceful toes and maybe a pinch of black hair on the surface for a second. She was gone!"

"You don't mean she drowned?" Lighthorse asked. The roll of sycamore bark had come apart in his hands.

"I didn't say that," Clem Philips said with a grin. "The Indians always said she was waiting for her true lover. And they went on to say she would drown anyone who tried to claim her, anyone not her true lover, that is."

"I wonder how her lover—did he have to do anything special to get her?"

"Oh no," Clem said with a chuckle, "nothing a true lover couldn't do. He just had to dive from the exact spot she dove from and swim underwater till he found her. Of course the river was at flood stage then, and the rock she dove from stands now about forty feet above the water and back some six or eight feet. I guess it'd take a pretty good man," Clem said. Then he added quickly, "Why you looking so glum, Lighthorse? Now don't tell me—now look here, young man, tell me exactly what's in your mind."

"I was just thinking—"

"You were just thinking that you're the best swimmer in Gnadenhutten—I know about you, Mister," Clem said severely. "I've seen you outdive and out-tag the whole town, but I don't want you trying some crazy stunt."

"Well, at least I'd be the other—" Lighthorse swept the little pile of bark aside.

"Man alive, of course you'd be true. But am I going to have to beat it into your head that this thing I've been telling you is just an old man's tale? A legend, boy, nothing but a legend."

"I could believe it. And if I ever had the chance, help it happen."

"Now you looky here, Lighthorse, I want no funny business—now or ever! Why, that's why I was telling you this story, so we could be man-to-man, not to have you go off getting yourself drowned and having your mom taking this damned bald scalp of mine that's not worth taking. Now you just forget about this—the whole kaboodle. I'm not too sure but what the man had to be an Indian anyhow." Clem Philips got up and drew his lawnmower toward him.

Lighthorse watched him, shrugged, smiled, and matched

his movement, and once more they mowed. When Clem hit a pine cone, wedging it between bar and blade, and got down on his knees to loosen it, Lighthorse was at his side in an instant.

"You know what I like about that story—the last one?"

"What?"

"It runs on—"

"Lighthorse!"

"It hasn't ended. I mean it runs on in my mind, and we're all in it. You and everyone in Gnadenhutten. I can imagine the whole thing like a moving picture, only better."

"Well, you be sure you just imagine it."

≫ 6 ≪

Now they went round and round the diminishing triangle of grass, Lighthorse a mower width to the left and eight feet to the rear of the old man. He watched Clem Philips' brown trousers move like the hind quarters of a toiling horse; he saw the cross of sweat beneath the old man's suspenders spread and darken the blue of his shirt; he grew weak and fuzzy in his own stomach, but still they followed the fading triangle as if chasing a green phantom that fled them as they moved. The grass triangle had become rug size when they heard the three long-drawn wails of the Biggers' Tile Factory whistle.

"There she goes," Clem Philips said. "Twelve o'clock noon comes none too soon. I'm a poet, and don't know it," he added, chuckling. He gave his mower a shove and let it flounder in the uncut grass. "Of course I can't afford to wish my life away, but lunch and quitting time never come too quick on this job. 'Hey Boy'," he called to Lighthorse, who was half listening but still mowing, "you can stop now and we'll eat a bite." He had pulled out his watch. "That damned whistle was six minutes late."

Lighthorse went ahead, bucking the mower against a heavy tuft of grass.

"Boy, did you hear me? Time to quit!" Clem fanned his hat at Lighthorse's back. "Your school buddy Ted Biggers just blew the Biggers' whistle behind time. Horace Biggers told me he paid Teddy a regular man's salary all summer just to blow that damned whistle and he blows it six minutes late."

Lighthorse sidestepped the hat as easily as he had sidestepped the head-down bull-like rushes of Ted Biggers on the playground. He said: "You forget, Clem, I'm to mow right through lunch—or else I'll owe you more money. That was our bargain." He made another charge at the green clump.

"Well, it seems I do recall some such agreement. Now if I was to break my half of the bargain—but of course you aren't at all hungry?"

"Not very," Lighthouse said through set lips.

"That's odd. I'd swear I heard your belly-button playing a tune on your backbone some ten minutes ago. But then you aren't hungry, you say?"

"No, heck no." Lighthorse wondered if he could hold his face in a grin until Clem looked away.

"Lighthorse, I'm going to tan the hide off your little rump if you keep lying to me." Clem Philips pulled Lighthorse away from his mower.

"Lying?" Lighthorse was twisting away.

"Lying! Lying! Not one hour ago you told me you wouldn't lie, and if you did you'd set it right, first off, and now—" Clem Philips grabbed Lighthorse and led him to where his aluminum dinner pail hung on a limb stump of the crab apple tree, and swung him aloft.

"If you must work, you can hand me my dinner bucket," he said. "Thanks. Now we'll see whether I raised my daughter to be a cook or a can-opener." He settled down, leaning back against the gnarled crab apple tree.

"Well, now look at that—I was hoping for loaves and fishes, but find only enough for two of us if we share a bit." Clem Philips smiled as he divided the two double swiss cheese sandwiches and laid the boiled egg beside the outmost pile. "And now you take your pick here," he said, lifting off the bottom section of the bucket and holding out a jar of sugared strawberries and a banana.

"I—I'd rather not eat."

"Of course you'd rather not eat. But just to punish you right I'm going to make you eat a sandwich and an egg and then those strawberries. Yes, sir, those strawberries will really get you down." Clem Philips caught the light in the blue eyes and smiled. "You know, Lighthorse Harry, you'll be known as Strawberry Harry in no time, and I'd like no guest better for lunch than Strawberry Harry."

"I'd still rather not eat." Lighthorse's eyes were nibbling at the sandwich on its way to Clem's mouth.

"Well"— Clem Philips bit largely and chewed—"can't say I blame you. This is the nearest thing to misery I can imagine."

"I could run home if I had to eat," Lighthorse said, squatting. "Mom might be expecting me. She was having beans —more navy beans and a ham bone."

"Yep—" Clem Philips caught up another bite, chewed and swallowed— "you could run home if you was absolutely set against being my guest at this picnic, and if you wanted that pile of food to go to waste." Again he sank his teeth into the quarter-inch slice of cheese with butter and relish between creamy homemade bread. "I reckon the ants and birds would like you for it too." He motioned toward the sandwich.

"Well—" Lighthorse's hand stole toward the sandwich as if he expected it to burn his fingers. "Well, I might try it." His hand closed around the bread.

"You'd better hurry, your mouth's already open."

≫ 7 ≪

Later, when only the banana skin lay like a collapsed umbrella before them, Clem Philips said: "Now that we've taken care of our common belly ache, we might just as well lie down on good Mother Earth." He grinned broadly and scraped together a pile of the newmown grass, tossed out a few twigs as undesirable, and lay back upon the green pillow, his straw hat covering his face. Once settled he peeked out from beneath the hat and said, "I always like to smell my own head—head smell is about all that keeps an old man from going back to the animals."

After a while Lighthorse went quietly to the pump, washed his hands and returned to shake a few ants off the strawberry jar, screw the lid on, and place the jar and spoon and banana skin in the dinner bucket. Then moving toward the deep snores, he pulled himself into the limbs to hang the bucket on the natural hook of the crab apple tree. Next he stood off to the side, listening to the rhythm of the snores and not knowing whether he dared go to the mower as he wished to do. He went—after waiting—and began to mow softly, so that the clack-clack only gradually replaced the rhythmic sound of the old man's breathing. He mowed quietly, doggedly, and soon he was far enough away to go flying at top speed, the tide of new strength from the best food he could remember having eaten carrying him along. He kept track of the rows he mowed—his mind was set on ten before Clem Philips awakened—and ten came and went, and twenty, and thirty and forty, and then he lost count. He was more than a hundred feet away from the crab tree at the nearest point and moving at a half run, moving in the flood tide of new-found strength when it occurred to him that Clem Philips was sleeping much too long.

He turned his head in sudden wonder—neither the head nor the arms nor legs had moved. Stone-age fear clawing him, he ran toward the old man. He stooped and listened above the straw hat, and even as he listened and watched for the rise and fall of the large chest beneath its blue covering, he realized that the chest had stopped its motion. And when he lifted the straw hat, he stared upon wide open brown eyes. Suddenly aware of the air and bird hush, and that he stood on sacred ground, he replaced the hat and set out on a dead run for home, dodging the blurred grey stones that rose like spirits around him.

PART TWO
1934

✑ 8 ✑

The new girl's hair ran down her back in two blue-black braids. The braids were tied in pink ribbons that matched her pink plaid jacket and skirt. Her eyes were dark gypsy pools in her olive face, and her teeth whiter than any teeth he had ever seen. But she didn't look at him, even though Lighthorse entered into the competition and threw his hand and leaped in his seat all during nine o'clock history class. He saw Miss Tillotson's intense blue eyes behind her glasses go wide in wonder, because she knew he knew the answers and she could call on him when the others ran out of answers. So she did, and he answered fully and precisely, but the new girl didn't pay the least attention.

And when Miss Tillotson was called from the room by Mr. Spiker, the principal—when Lighthorse should have found some way of gaining the new girl's attention, of learning her name and where she was living and all he had to know—he didn't get a chance. The moment Miss Tillotson closed the door, Ted Biggers claimed the attention of the dark gypsy eyes. He reached into the rats' nest of paper, pencils, string, and broken pen knives inside his desk, fumbled, cried out in pain, and then held up a thumb split by a razor blade. The blade still hung upon the thumb, down which poured a red stream.

Naturally she—whoever she was—gasped her sympathy, and then her wonder! For Ted Biggers calmly caught the razor blade between his teeth and pulled it from his thumb; he wiped the red ink off on his shirt-tail, and held up the uninjured thumb and the razor blade that had a piece chipped out so it would fit neatly between nail and flesh.

She laughed with Ted Biggers then, joyously, and Lighthorse wondered what the consequences would be if he drove his steel pen into Ted Biggers' sturdy back and brought forth real blood.

Her interest secure, Ted Biggers grinned broadly as he doubled an eighteen-inch piece of string, knotted the ends, unbuttoned his shirt, and slid the knotted string through the button hole, hooked it with thumb and forefinger on each side, and said, "See!" His fingers loosened but the string didn't come loose and he pretended to be disappointed. Again he said, "See!" and, quicker than the eye, let go with both fingers and one thumb; caught the loop with the falling thumb; lengthened the loop; and thus—miraculously, it appeared—extracted the string from the buttonhole. Lighthorse saw dark eyes dancing as Miss Tillotson came in and called the class to order.

"We now have the pleasure of attending the special assembly previously announced in your homeroom," Miss Tillotson said. "Mr. Spiker has arranged that all classes will gather in the auditorium for a short but most significant program. Go quietly, please." As she spoke, Miss Tillotson turned an adoring gaze upon Lighthorse, and he shook his head, blushing. Even as he wished Miss Tillotson would look away, or that the pink girl—she was exotic in pink— would look his way, Lighthorse heard Ted Biggers whisper close to her ear, "Ever see a brown-nosed teacher's pet?"

In the outpouring at the bell, Lighthorse got near enough to swing at Ted Biggers. They would have gone round and round, as they had done in the past, since Ted Biggers was heavier and no coward, but Mr. Spiker caught them at the door. He grabbed Lighthorse's yellow hair and Ted Biggers' brown hair in his strong fists and knocked both heads against the wall. "What's going on here? Looking for trouble? Kind of roughing it, eh?" he growled down upon them.

"Nope," Lighthorse said. "I just swatted at a beetle flying out the door."

"A what?" Mr. Spiker exclaimed.

"I think he means a body louse, a bedbug, sir." Ted Biggers picked at Lighthorse's collar and examined the nothing he found.

Lighthorse was aflame now that the new girl stood against the far window, her face glowing with wonder and affection as she looked past him to Ted Biggers.

"Aw, get on your way," Mr. Spiker said to Ted Biggers, letting him escape to the new girl's side.

"And you, Lighthorse—I'm doubly ashamed of you," Mr. Spiker said. "You know how much we've all come to expect from you—and I'm about to say it all in public."

"Why should you—" Lighthorse began, but he mumbled apology as Mr. Spiker patted his shoulder and then nudged him into the stream of passing students.

When the auditorium was filled and the noise had died to an ear-tickling buzz, "The Star Spangled Banner" was played by a six-piece combo directed by Percy Renwick, the music and mathematics teacher, whose geometric gestures in conducting earned him the nickname "The Puppet." After Percy Renwick took his bow, Mr. Spiker, tall and athletic and just slightly bald above a face focused on a large Roman nose, walked to the lectern. The entire auditorium grew strangely quiet, for Mr. Spiker moved with a briskness out of keeping with his ordinary gait.

"Students of Gnadenhutten-Clay Township Schools," he began. He waited, repeated the salutation, and said: "I have called a special assembly at this time to speak to all of you —both grade and high school students—on what is our primary purpose in this school, in all education, I might add: scholarly performance and attainment." A slight noise, barely identifiable as a groan, arose from the audience. "Yes," Mr. Spiker went on in his nasal twang, "so often we assemble here for other purposes, purposes only remotely connected with our primary objective—for pep rallies." The stomping of feet and a raucous "Sis, boom, bah, G.H.S. rah, rah, rah!" echoed from the upper balcony, where Hank and Hubert and a dozen of their buddies occupied the top-most row. Mr. Spiker waited patiently and then said: "We meet here for school drives of one sort or another, oftentimes for praiseworthy purposes, I must add, but not to be confused with our primary purpose. Our primary purpose is of course one thing: education."

A rising moan overtook his words; again he waited. "Today I have called a special assembly to announce a special honor that has come to several from our midst and to one person in particular." All noise died, for Mr. Spiker had reached in his inside coat pocket for a paper and had found it missing. "Now what did I do with that pesky list?" He felt in the side pockets of his gray suit, even explored his hip pockets and then studied the floor he had traversed to reach the lectern. "Well, doesn't that beat all get out!" he exclaimed, and the twitter became a roar, a roar that included all the teachers except Miss Tillotson, who stood straight and severe, her eyes focused on Lighthorse, bathing him in an all but holy light.

"Well, Charlie, you did it again," Mr. Spiker said, speaking of himself to himself. "You've lost the list of the scores of your students." When the laughter subsided, he said to the audience, "Forgive the soliloquy. Perhaps my memory will suffice. . . ."

"Sir," Ted Biggers called out, rising, silencing the hall and stepping forward from the second row of seats, glancing over his shoulder as he did so to make certain that the new girl watched his every move. "Sir, perhaps I could be of some help. I noticed this paper on the floor—just outside our door where you so often stand as classes change."

Mr. Spiker's eyes identified the neatly folded paper in Ted Biggers' hand; now they narrowed and focused intensely for a moment, but only a moment. Smiling, he went forward to meet Ted Biggers, to take the list. "Thank you, Ted," he said. "That was gross carelessness on my part."

"Not at all, not at all," Ted Biggers said, as he bowed to the applause and held up a neat finger circle signifiying to the students a deed carried off to absolute perfection.

"Now let us continue," Mr. Spiker said returning to the lectern and trying to regain his enthusiasm. But the sighs of the students, the lead feel of the air, and the shifting of restless feet told everyone that the climactic moment had come and gone—at least Lighthorse read the signs this way —and a dozen students certified his judgment as they ignored Mr. Spiker and reached out to touch Ted Biggers' arm as he entered the third row of seats and deliberately swung his legs across the back of his seat to regain his place beside the new girl.

Amid broken volleys of applause Mr. Spiker now read off six names and delivered certificates, to each boy and girl in the sophomore, junior, and senior classes who had scored highest in the annual achievement test required of all students at the Gnadenhutten–Clay Township Senior High School. Lighthorse slumped lower and lower in his seat, so low that he had to be prodded out when Mr. Spiker announced that one student, a junior high boy he had permitted to take the test, had achieved not only the highest score in the school but the highest in all of Tuscarawas County. After he added that he could have remembered this fact without his list, Mr. Spiker said, "I'm sure I need not tell most of you, that student is Harry Clark Lee, known to us as Lighthorse. And I want him to stand for a round of well-earned recognition as I hand him this certificate."

When Lighthorse got to his feet, his lips shaped the single word "junk," for he realized that this was applause generated from above, altogether unlike the spontaneous wave that had arisen for Ted Biggers, and his humiliation was complete when Miss Tillotson strode forward to help Mr. Spiker summon acclaim for her prize student. Standing for the moment, robbed of glory before he had it, Lighthorse noticed that the new girl wasn't even looking in his direction. Her head of dark braids was bent toward Ted Biggers as they laughed over some private joke.

❧ 9 ❧

One purpose was served by the "missionary meeting for our scholar," as Ted Biggers named it. Its close permitted Lighthorse to learn that the new girl—her full name was Nancy *Lee* Sutton—had moved into a brick mansion at the other end of Walnut Street from the little Lee house, and that her father was president of the Tuscora Bank, which had undergone reorganization and was once again open for business.

So sour was the honor award for him that Lighthorse was caught unawares by his mother's action at the supper table. She waited until the family was seated and Mr. Lee had returned thanks with the sing-song voice he used in anything that smelled of religion, a holdover from the years he had served as a Methodist circuit rider before a conflict with the Church Board forced him into what Mrs. Lee always called his "Public Works," his present job as section hand for the Pennsylvania Railroad. Once Grace had been spoken and the plates filled, Mrs. Lee stood up and drew Lighthorse's head against her breast as she announced to her husband, "Nat, you'll never guess what happened at school today."

"Now what?" Mr. Lee glanced quickly at Lighthorse and then at Hubert to gauge what effect his remark might have. "I hope you're not following in Hubert's footsteps. I just got his window paid for."

"No broken windows this time." Mrs. Lee's fingers lingered on Lighthorse's head as he shook off her embrace.

"You selling shampoo or something?" Lighthorse matched his mother's beaming face and felt the warmth of pleasure grip him.

"What happens at Gnaden–Clay School is soon forgotten," Hank announced.

"Old times there are soon forgotten," Lighthorse sang.

"You tell us what happened, Hubert," Mrs. Lee said.

"What the deuce happened?" Ed asked.

"Yeah, what the hell happened?" Elmo repeated. Elmo, who had once turned down a scholarship at Ohio State University because the family needed his paycheck, was already talking of his plans for Lighthorse—anything so Lighthorse could avoid the back-breaking labor Elmo had to do, in his new job firing kilns and loading sewer pipe at the Biggers' Tile Factory.

"Well, we had a special assembly for one thing," Hessie said, speaking to them all but looking at her father. "We had a special assembly, Dad, and Mr. Spiker made a little speech and he didn't say anything mean about one of your boys this time."

"He didn't because he couldn't," Lighthorse said. "Nosey Spiker lost his lousy set speech."

"Sure, Dad," Hessie said. "I got to see it—the whole school got to see it—and Mr. Spiker was awfully funny."

"He lost his crappy little list or something," Hubert said, "but he sure unloaded his usual forkful of horse manure."

"A spreader full!" Hank exclaimed. "We smelled it in the balcony where us regulars get to sit."

"You regulars sometimes misspell S-I-T," Elmo said.

"Wasn't that Ted Biggers acting crazy?" Hessie said.

"Hey—to save a lost sinner, tell me what happened," Mr. Lee said. "What did *you* do, Lighthorse?"

Lighthorse looked at his father and then at his mother. He couldn't keep his pleasure from his face, but it wasn't his story to tell. "I just listened, Dad. And like Hessie said, Ted Biggers made Nosey Spiker look like an idiot."

"Hessie, dear, you tell us what happened," Mr. Lee said.

"Well, Mr. Spiker called this special assembly and said it was to give credit to those who did well in the annual intelligence test. He read off the winners in each class—"

"He forgot Hube and me," Hank interrupted, laughing. "The scores don't run high enough."

"To reach the balcony—where you regulars sit?" Elmo asked.

"Spelled S-I-T," Lighthorse whispered to Everett.

Hessie exclaimed: "But he didn't forget Lighthorse!"

"Oh, he wouldn't forget your peerless little Lighthouse," Hubert went on. "He said our beaming bright light made the best score in the whole school, and not only that, but the best score in Tuscarawas County."

"In the whole damn county!" Elmo said, reaching across Ed to whack Lighthorse on the shoulder. "Hey buddy, that's all right!"

"By God, that's showing 'em!" Everett exclaimed.

"Well, Son," Mr. Lee said, stretching out his hand and then dropping it because he couldn't reach Lighthorse, "you're certainly to be congratulated! In fact"—he glanced at his wife to see what offer the family budget could stand —"in fact, I'd say we'll just make a little appreciation offer of our own." His eyes gathered assent from Elmo and Everett

49

and from the unemployed Ed. "We'll just give you any little gift you'd like to have, won't we, boys? Now Lighthorse, you name it and we'll give it to you."

"You mean it?" Lighthorse said. "You really mean it?"

"You're damned right we mean it!" Elmo said. He turned and got a nod from Everett.

"You name something within reason and the boys and I'll see that you get it," Mr. Lee said. "How about a fountain pen or a good Ingersoll pocket watch?"

"A good Ingersoll with a shoestring for a chain?" Hank asked Ed.

"No." Lighthorse looked at his plate, pried at the edge of the plate with his fork. "I would like one thing, though." He turned to his mother. "Mom, if it's just the same to you, I'd sure like for you *not* to take in Mr. Sutton's washing if he asks you." Lighthorse heard the silence—felt it—and looked from one face to another.

"Oh brother!" Hank cried. "Now I know why Lighthorse thought Ted Biggers stole the whole damned show."

"Yippee!" Hubert cried. "Meet the great lover Lee!"

"Boy, are you red," Hessie said to Lighthorse. "Your ears are burning."

Hank began to sing, and Hubert and Ed joined him:

"And the moon shines bright on pretty Redwing,
Whose heart is aching. . . ."

"Hank, Hubert, Ed, can it!" Mr. Lee ordered. "Now please—please tell me what is going on. Who is Mr. Sutton? What's young Biggers got to do with it?" He addressed his wife, but Mrs. Lee was looking at Lighthorse, with tears forming in her eyes.

"Mr. Sutton is the new president of the bank," she explained as she rubbed her eyes with the back of her hand. "He took Vic Kellogg's place. They just last weekend moved into the Kellogg house. And—" She looked at Lighthorse, shaking her head.

"But what's important," Hubert said, "is that there's a girl named Nancy—a dark-haired sparkler—in Lighthorse's class, and Ted Biggers has her falling for his line."

"She looks cute—real cute," Hessie said. "Is she part Spanish or something?"

"Now I know why Lighthorse didn't like the way Ted Biggers made a fool out of old Nosey Spiker," Hubert said. "Everyone else thought the program was okay for a crappy thing like that—everyone except Lighthorse, I guess."

"Lighthorse—Lighthorse, I just don't know what to make of you," Mr. Lee said. "One minute I hear you're the genius of the county and the next moment you're the Rudolph Valentino. Now if I could . . ." He cleared his throat and silenced the wisecracks the others were making. "A promise is a promise, and we'll still give you your request. Mary," he said solemnly, "no matter how many dollars Mr. Sutton offers per shirt I think you can tell him you've got all the laundry business you. . ."

"But I can't," Mrs. Lee said, rubbing at her forehead. "Mr. Sutton's shirts are in the tub soaking at this moment."

"Quiet—you Hank—Hubert! All of you, shut up!" Mr. Lee tried to still the family riot.

He looked around the table. "All right, Lighthorse, we'll do the next best thing on our award. Since Hank and Hubert get so much fun out of this Nancy Sutton, they'll both want to meet her often. Well, we'll let 'em. Hank, I want you to take this week's wash back to the Suttons' when it's ready. Hubert, you'll take the next one. Then Hank, it'll be your turn again, and so on." Mr. Lee looked at Elmo and

Ed and Everett who were sharing some private joke. "What's that, Elmo?"

"Ev was just saying it might even turn out that Hank or Hubert would see a familiar face on a guest in the Sutton house—what then?"

"He might even answer the door," Everett said. "You know a young man likes to make himself useful." He winked at his mother. "I always do."

"Good! Dandy!" Mr. Lee said. "Hank, if you or Hubert ever meet someone who *might* look like your brother Lighthorse when you go to deliver the laundry, I want it strictly understood that your vision is faulty. You're not to speak to him."

"Couldn't I say 'Here's your Poppa-in-law's filthy underwear and his stinking socks, clean and neat, sir?' " Hubert asked.

"How'd you like a *pair* of socks—in the eye?" Lighthorse said.

"You'd better save that for Ted Biggers," Hank said to Lighthorse. "One of these times he's going to whip you."

"Sure he will—but only if fists full of dollars weigh more than flesh and blood and bone," Lighthorse said.

"I don't get it," Everett said, glancing at Hank and Ed who matched his look.

"Lighthorse, you're rightly named for a revolutionist," Elmo said. He went on, "Dad, did I ever tell you what Ted Biggers said down at the swimming hole about fighting Lighthorse? He told me he didn't want to whip Lighthorse. . ."

"Because he can't," Lighthorse said.

"He didn't want to whip Lighthorse because he'd have to fight Hube, and then if he whipped Hube, he'd have to fight Hank, and then Ev, and then Ed, and then *me*. He said, 'It's not fair that the Lees come in a clan,' and I said, 'You speak to your old man and old woman on that one.' "

"Hey, this young Biggers may be wiser than you've led me to think," Mr. Lee said.

"Maybe Ted Biggers can't fight—I guess I shouldn't say that either," Lighthorse said. "Well, whether he can fight or not, he's clever enough to pick a paper out of Nosey Spiker's inside pocket while old Nosey's busy shaking him."

"While Nosey Spiker is busy shaking who?" Hank asked.

"I thought I saw a fair-haired bugger about your size in his left hand—I'm not allowed to see *Lighthorse*, you know," he added significantly to his father.

"Is that another story or was that the way Mr. Spiker chose to examine your intelligence?" Mr. Lee asked.

"He just bumped their heads gently against the wall to make sure which was emptiest," Hubert said. "Lighthorse won."

"Everything is nothing—nothing at all," Lighthorse said, nodding to Hubert, acknowledging his stroke. To Elmo he said: "You know how old Nosey Spiker always imagines somebody is fighting, when somebody is simply helping somebody else keep from falling down."

"Now I know," Hubert said. "I'll never see Lighthorse on the Sutton front porch, but I may see 'a somebody.' "

"Probably Ted Biggers," Hank said.

"We'll see what *you* see," Lighthorse said.

"Now I get it," Mr. Lee said. "This young Biggers stole a paper from Mr. Spiker's pocket, eh? Now let me tell you three boys something: he may be clever and he may be having a lot of fun, but right there's where I want you Lee boys to back-water. You hear that, Lighthorse? And you too, Hank and Hubert?"

"Yes sir, Mr. Gandy Dancer," Hank said. With muscles set he lunged up and down in his chair as if tamping railroad ties.

"I heard you, Mr. G. D.," Hubert said.

"That comes out: 'Gee-Dee-Na-than-ee-el Lee'," Lighthorse sang, winking at his father. "By the way, Mom," he added, "I've been thinking a little about that Sutton laundry, and I'm glad you're going to be doing it."

"It'll be done right!" Mr. Lee announced.

"Yes—and I'm going to take it back," Lighthorse said, looking at Hank.

"You won't have to fight me for the stinking job," Hank said. "If I wanted to see Nancy Sutton, I'd see her without a basket of laundry for an excuse."

"Nancy's cute and different. She's tall too," Hessie explained to Everett and Ed.

"Maybe I *will* decide I want to pull her pigtails," Hank said. "She's a little young, but—"

"Shut up, Hank," Mrs. Lee said.

"Let him talk," Lighthorse said. "With winter coming, we need all the hot air we can generate."

≥ 10 ≤

Tuesday evening, while his mother moved back and forth from back porch to kitchen and from ironing board to the three large wicker laundry baskets, slowly filling them with neatly ironed, fresh-smelling clothes, Lighthorse sat in the darkened living room, running his fingers aimlessly up and down the worn cords that stuck through the sides of the sofa. Once or twice he was ready to go to his mother, but each time he changed his mind before he left the shadow of the room. Finally he went, still uncertain, but ready in Hessie's absence to help pack clothes and by action clear his mind.

"Sutton shirt—Sutton scarf—Arkwright tablecloth—all these are Arkwright—and these are Peterson," Mrs. Lee said. "No, the third basket. That's right, those are Sutton napkins, this is a Sutton slip and undershirt—they go on bottom, ironed things on top. One thing I'll tell you about the Suttons right now," Mrs. Lee said, "they buy quality, even where it doesn't show. I always like to feel that about people," she added. "Careful, those are Mr. Sutton's shirts."

"That's all?" Lighthorse asked, laying on the last neatly folded shirt.

"That's all—good," Mrs. Lee said. "Now hand me a paper—goodness, not newspaper. Do you want to ruin a hard day's work? Never put newspaper near clean clothes. I'd rather try to wash out street dirt than newsprint."

Lighthorse handed her a brown laundry paper and said, "Mom, I'd like to talk to you a little bit, could I?"

"I've been running within speaking range for some minutes," his mother said. Then she caught a glimpse of his face, pushed back her loosened hair and followed him into the darkened room. She sat in the chair facing the sofa, but she made no effort to turn on a lamp.

"There's just one thing I wanted to say." Lighthorse found comfort in the darkness and the sound of his mother's deep breathing—she *had* been running from cellar to kitchen. "I don't want you to misunderstand all that crap last night at the table. Most of all, what I said about you taking in the Sutton's laundry."

"I think I understand."

"You know how it is—I mean how it was, at first. I just knew they'd bring their laundry here, and that was something I couldn't bear—I mean for you and us to have to do their laundry, and then have them think that we were just people who did other people's laundry. You know what I mean?"

Mrs. Lee's hand reached toward his hand, but she got up and sat beside him without touching him. "Of course I know, Lighthorse."

"I was all set to apologize for all of us—when I came home from school. You know how it is when we never have much and I'm wearing the same clothes Hank and Hubert wore and people are handing out that crap like 'those pants shine like they been sitting in this grade before' and 'the shirt is familiar, even if the face isn't.'"

"That sounds like something Ted Biggers might say."

"He says it, but plenty of others say the same things—only he says it better than most. Well, I was thinking about that and us all afternoon, and I just didn't see how I could stay in this town if you took in the Sutton laundry."

"Oh, Lighthorse."

"I know it was just crap, but I thought it."

"I don't mean that, not at all, Lighthorse." Mrs. Lee's voice changed. "I hope you also know you've said 'crap' about twenty times the last couple days."

"That's a big pile, eh?" Lighthorse laughed. "Thanks. But what I thought was that too." He paused. "I was pretty desperate, and when Dad made his offer I just tried to get away with something, something I didn't really want when I said it. And then after I said it and saw how it hurt you and Dad—sure I saw that, I'd have been blind not to—and after I heard Elmo and Ed and Everett, yes, and Hank and Hube and Hessie—when I heard all of you stick up for all of us, *including me* when I was like that—well, I just wanted you to know." Lighthorse cleared his throat.

Mrs. Lee's hand touched his; her fingers did a quick dance up his arm.

After a moment Lighthorse said, "Do you think Dad and the others understand about the laundry—understand why I'm taking it?"

"They'd better! Of course they do. By the way, the last thing Dad said last night was that he was real proud of you, Lighthorse. He said you are different—well, what he meant was you've got to accept suffering, maybe more than most. He knows what he's talking about too, for you know how

57

he always sacrificed himself for his brothers, and how he tried to educate and lead that narrow-minded bunch of church mannequins, and failed. And today he's a better man than most ministers even if he doesn't preach. And that he failed isn't too important. What is important is that he tried. He tried—and with *us* he succeeded. Not many women can say that after thirty-two years when they've had seven children by a man, not when they take in washings to help eke out a poor living."

"I know. God, how I know it."

There was a silence. Finally Lighthorse blew his nose and said, "I'd better take that laundry back now."

≥ I I ≤

After nightfall the temperature had fallen rapidly, and with wind-driven snow pelting his face, his hands cracked and numbing against the steel tongue of the battered red wagon with its high-stacked wicker basket, Lighthorse walked with one goal in mind: to make it to the nearest tree, a small seedling plum whose fruit had never been deemed worth picking so it hung like burned out ornaments upon the wind-tossed limbs. At that tree he set as his goal the next plum, and the next, and the next—seven in all. So he made his way up the slippery path in the field opposite the John E. Heckewelder Moravian Church, to pass the first of the town's five street lights, swaying on screeching wires.

At the end of the Tillotson garden the path became one of packed ashes, and he stopped there to stomp the clinging mud off his tennis shoes. By standing on his numbed toes and kicking into the ashes, he rid his shoes of most of the mud and water. Then he pulled the creaking wagon, along the ash path beneath the three sugar maples, to the corner of Walnut and Main, and continued—now on a concrete walk—along Walnut. He passed the Tuscora Bank, on the corner opposite Jumper's Store; Shoenfelder's Drug Store; Lemon's Grocery; Hartley's Barber Shop; the Busy Bee Store; Holder's Hardware; the Gnadenhutten Post Office— in a partitioned area of the Hardware—and Bird's Confectionery.

He picked up his pace once he was past the lighted storefronts—he had walked slowly and nonchalantly there— and the wagon wheels with bearings missing thumped over the alternating cement and brick sidewalk, which lay level to the Methodist parsonage and then fell away several blocks to where Walnut Street crossed Route 36.

At the last house before the west turn of Route 36, a large brick two-story mansion set well back in a yard of maples and beeches, damp black and grey against the reflected light, his pace slowed. Before he turned in, he stopped to brush off snow and make sure the laundry basket was upright, the protective paper and load intact. When he had followed the walk to the long front porch, he stopped again. This time he stepped into the sleety grass and wiped his shoes carefully, stooping to pry out the frozen mud with his fingers. He wiped his hands in the grass and then along his pants, tucked in his shirt tail, flipped his hands several times through his soggy hair and dried them on the inside of his corduroy jacket. Next he blew on his hands, brushed the snow off the top of the laundry paper, and lifted the basket of clothes from the wagon. He remembered to be careful of the loose right handle, and remembered to hold the high-stacked wicker basket well out from his damp body. He got the basket onto the porch, stepped around it, again blew on his stinging hands, and then laid one finger against the white enameled bell ringer that moved in and out on a spring.

Shivering, he waited, then rang a second time, and a third.

The notes of a piano—sounding too distant to be in the first room—rushed out to meet him as the door opened slightly.

"Mrs. Sutton, I—" his voice faltered. He was not prepared for the perfume and jewelry worn by the tall, dark-haired woman, clad in a red wool dress and high heels.

"Yes, what is it?"

"Mrs. Sutton, I've brought the laundry Mr. Sutton left at our house yesterday. He said you needed it as soon as possible and Mom just got it done."

"Oh, you're the laundry boy." Mrs. Sutton swung the door just far enough for Lighthorse to glimpse a large square living room which centered on a stone fireplace. Her braceleted arm was pointing to the walk that ran to the left of the porch toward the adjoining three-car garage. "You just take our laundry into the garage, and I'll have Mr. Sutton take care of it tomorrow."

"I think clothes—newly washed clothes—" Lighthorse said, intending to explain that it wasn't a good idea to store newly ironed clothes in a garage all night, even if the garage had a cement floor.

But Mrs. Sutton interrupted: "Please leave the laundry there the next time without ringing."

"I don't think there'll be—" Lighthorse began, but he was talking to the solid oak door and he did not finish. He turned toward the laundry basket and felt an overwhelming desire to charge it head-on, to kick and trample it about the porch and into the mud. "Boy," he said to the laundry basket, "isn't she something!" As an afterthought he added, now that he knew how tough he could be, "Hell's bells, ain't we something?"

He shoved the laundry basket clear of the door, turned and walked off the porch, caught the wagon, snapped it around and set off on a dead run. The careening wagon banged him on the back of the heels every three or four steps, but he was too hot to notice, too hot to feel the sleety snow pelting down.

❧ 12 ❦

By the time Lighthorse passed the Methodist parsonage, he had settled down to a walk, and at the outset of the four or five lighted store fronts he was barely moving. In the brightest light of all, in front of Shoenfelder's Drug Store, he stopped and peered long at his face in the lighted window. Then, aware that he was shivering, his teeth chattering, he turned the wagon around. Slowly at first and then with the speed of absolute determination he retraced the blocks to the red brick mansion.

Once more he parked the wagon against the stone step and moved to the heavy front door. This time he ignored the enameled bell with its civilized jingle; instead he folded his fist and struck rapid blows, blows that brought immediate results, for the massive door opened while his fist was still in motion.

"I just wanted to tell you you can take your wash and. . ." He gulped, and then said in a voice gone suddenly off key, "You aren't—are you Mr. Sutton?"

"I am, but I'm not sure I want to admit it," replied the short bald man clad in dungarees and a blue turtleneck sweater. "Tell you what," he added, grinning, "you unfold your fist and I'll let you call me Clarence. Clarence," he commanded as he drew Lighthorse into the brightly lighted room and closed the door, "Clarence, you billiard ball," he barked into the corner of the room, "show that young man in." He straightened his face, bowed, and said solemnly, "This way, right this way, sir." And in a low whisper, "By the way, what was your name?"

"I'm Harry Lee," Lighthorse said. "I'm called Light-horse," he added vaguely as he felt himself floating across a red pile rug to stand before the gleaming expanse of the first grand piano he had ever seen. "My mother does your laundry—that Lee, I mean." Lighthorse was aware that *she* was wearing a housecoat of yellow velvet.

"Miss Nancy Sutton, may I present Lighthorse Harry Lee."

"We've met," Nancy Sutton said, holding up her hand, and then suddenly seizing Lighthorse's in a workaday grip. "Pop, you stinker," she went on, "Lighthorse and I happen to be classmates—almost friends. In fact," she laughed, "I was hoping he'd come by sometime and tell me how to keep from failing that pre-algebra or whatever 'The Puppet' Renwick calls it."

"God, I hope he *will*—I can't," Mr. Sutton said. Nancy sat down and motioned Lighthorse toward a chair. Lighthorse looked at his feet and the rug but Mr. Sutton had him by the arm and there was no turning back.

The three of them settled in a triangle near the log fire; they talked about the weather, arithmetic and banking, and music. Later, when Nancy went to the kitchen to prepare hot chocolate and cookies, Mr. Sutton got up and said to

Lighthorse, "You mentioned the laundry—your mother hasn't got it done already?"

Lighthorse felt green about the mouth. "She did it this morning, ironed it tonight. It's on the porch." He got up and moved to open the door.

"How nice—you thank her, for I needed my shirts and Selma needed the linen." Mr. Sutton touched the light switch. "Here, I'll help you with the basket." Between them they brought the basket into the center of the living room. "You didn't carry this up the steps by yourself?"

"I'm not too sure I carried it," Lighthorse said. "I'm more the dragging type."

"It doesn't look dragged to me," Mr. Sutton said. "Nancy —Nancy," he called, "break a couple of eggs in that chocolate, Lighthorse here has done a day's work." He lifted off the paper to get at his shirts. "Now that looks exactly the way I want a shirt to look."

"Mom's the best washer in town."

"So I heard," Mr. Sutton said. "By the way, that being best in town—even in the county—must sort of run in your family."

"Did *she*?" Lighthorse motioned toward the kitchen.

"Did she tell me!" Mr. Sutton said. "She hasn't talked anything else for the past two days. And she isn't exactly a harum-scarum herself," he added. "Except for arithmetic or pre-algebra, or whatever they call it."

"Quit talking about my weaknesses," Nancy said as she brought the tray with three cups of steaming chocolate into the room.

"I was talking about Lighthorse basically."

Nancy looked at Lighthorse and it seemed to him that her dark eyes registered a question. She served the chocolate and her father said: "Something warm for the belly and soft for the ears. What better combination could one wish for?" He stretched out before the fire and asked Nancy to play the piano.

Lighthorse moved to the fire, his back against a red and black leather hassock, and as the notes of the sweetest music he had ever heard filled the room, it seemed to him that he must be dreaming. Years before, returning from Jumper's Store in midwinter, he had fallen in the snow and had lain in a stupor until he was blessedly warm—running naked through knee-high cornfields to play with Hubert and Hank on the sunny green bank of the Tuscarawas River—and only Elmo's finding him had saved his life. Now he must have stumbled and fallen along the way to deliver the Sutton laundry, he had fallen and only his mind had carried him to the fire in the oak paneled room, to the pleasant drone of Mr. Sutton's voice and to the faint far music from *her* fingers.

Fearful that he was dreaming, Lighthorse edged a hand toward the twig at the end of the apple log that sizzled with fragrant juices. The twig touched between thumb and finger, touched and clung. Lighthorse shook the brand from his fingers and glanced toward Mr. Sutton. Mr. Sutton had been studying the fire with his eyes half-closed, but Lighthorse realized his action had been seen. He raised the burned finger to his mouth. "Apple—applewood."

Mr. Sutton said, "I pruned at the trees out back, and Nancy built the fire."

They turned toward Nancy. Her whipping braids told them she had suddenly found it necessary to give her full attention to Chopin.

❧ 13 ❧

The homeward walk, filled with waits in the tree shadows to trap snow in his open mouth, and quick starts that threatened to tear the tongue out of the wagon, seemed all downhill. With difficulty Lighthorse kept his feet on the ground. But for the wagon he sensed that he would rise and fly, and so he did at long last, two bounds to clear the porch once he had sent the wagon careening to park between the porch and angle of snow that marked the doors of the outside cellarway. Aware how the Lee and Sutton worlds clashed, and committed to reconciling them, come what might, he crossed the dining room to the kitchen before he realized that the family—his mother and father, Hessie, Hubert, and Hank—were gathered in emergency session in the small front room. The acrid stench of vomit hit him hard, and he pushed past Hubert and Hank to see Everett and Ed stretched full length on the opened davenport. "Drunk—are they drunk?" he whispered to his father who knelt rubbing at the rug and then dipped his towel in the scrub bucket to rub again.

"They're sick!" Mrs. Lee said. She used a wet towel to wipe away the vomit that dribbled from Ed's half-opened mouth.

"They're dead drunk—if you ask me."

"Nobody asked you, young man," Mr. Lee said, lifting his head to fix Lighthorse with cold blue eyes. "Mary," he said to his wife, "I wish to god you'd get those kids to bed, no need to have the whole house jammed in this one room."

"I'd just as soon they see it," Mrs. Lee said angrily. "Maybe if you and I had come in a few times like this, Ed and Everett wouldn't be here now." She rubbed her hand across her nose and Lighthorse saw that she had been crying.

"Now, Mary," Mr. Lee said. "Mary, you know we're not responsible for this."

"Well, I'd like to meet the one who is," Mrs. Lee said as she went toward the kitchen.

"Hey, somebody's in a car outside," Hank called out as he moved toward the front door. "Uh-oh, there's two of 'em. Hey Dad," he called from the porch, "I think you'd better come here. It's Elmo, and it looks like—yep, he's plastered."

"You just open the door, my boy," Lighthorse heard a newly familiar voice say. "That's fine."

"Dad—Dad, it's Mr. Sutton," Lighthorse whispered from the living room doorway. "And he's got Elmo with him —and Elmo's drunk."

"Good evening, Mr. Lee," Mr. Sutton said, "and hello again, Lighthorse. That's it, you just take his other arm." He looked knowingly at Mr. Lee and said, "Maybe we could stow him in the other room—"

"Mercy no, not there," Mrs. Lee said, reaching behind her to close the door to the front room; Lighthorse got there first.

"Here, Hessie, you bring some blankets—we'll put him

68

right here beside the table. It's warmer here," Mrs. Lee explained to Mr. Sutton.

Hubert said: "Ed and Everett are—"

"Hubert!" Mr. Lee said sharply. "Would you please go and help Hessie with the blankets."

"I've already got them—all that Everett and Ed aren't using," Hessie called as she tripped down from upstairs. "They're dead drunk—out cold in the front room," she said severely to Mr. Sutton.

"Uh—well," Mr. Sutton said, "I'm sure we've all had that experience—us men, I mean."

"Yes, that's right," Mr. Lee said. He and Mr. Sutton exchanged glances, as they laid Elmo out like an oversized doll and curled him slightly to fit the corner.

"You've got six sons then," Mr. Sutton said as he knelt to loosen Elmo's left shoe. Lighthorse was loosening the right shoe, and Mr. Lee was undoing his tie and shirt.

"Here, I can do that," Mrs. Lee said to Mr. Sutton.

"There are six of us boys, but Dad only lets us do things by threes," Lighthorse said to Mr. Sutton. He felt sick, and wondered if he looked it.

"Where'd you find Elmo?" Hank asked, but Mr. Sutton was saying, "It's sensible to do things by threes when you're six, I think."

"Things like this at least." Mr. Lee unfastened Elmo's belt, and then pulled the cover up and tucked it around his shoulders.

Mrs. Lee had disappeared into the front room, but now she reappeared and left the door open. "Won't you join us for a cup of coffee?" she asked Mr. Sutton. "I've got a pot started."

"Well yes," Mr. Sutton said. "I would like a cup of coffee, if you can stand my at-home uniform." He threw off his scarf and overcoat to reveal the dungarees and turtle neck sweater Lighthorse had seen earlier, and the others moved with him to the kitchen. Seated opposite the large coal stove, a cup of coffee on his knee, with Hubert and Hessie and Lighthorse slipping in and out, Mr. Sutton said, "It's certainly a fine family you've got, Mr. Lee."

"I think so," Mr. Lee said. "But I won't ask Mary to confirm it at this moment."

"Well—" she turned from the stove to see if he were joking, "I guess there's always a first time for everything. Leave that front room door open, Hank," she called. She turned to Mr. Sutton. "I don't know how to say it—but whatever the human race seems capable of, we manage to do it."

"The human race should apologize to God for His creating chaos with rotten apples in this Garden of Eden?" Mr. Lee asked. Lighthorse saw that his father's lips were in the prim line he reserved for irony.

"I'd settle for that," Mr. Sutton said, nodding. "And we don't need to apologize. Boys will be boys, and fermented apple juice is hard cider, as my uncle Joshua used to say."

"You think it was hard cider?" Mr. Lee asked. "I don't know much about liquor but I think anyone might get a little too much hard cider in a town like Gnadenhutten. I remember my brothers—"

"Nat," Mrs. Lee said, "we've got troubles enough. Forget your brothers."

"Well I can speak of a problem nearer home," Mr. Sutton said in a low voice.

Mr. and Mrs. Lee looked at him.

"Mrs. Sutton," he said quietly. "And not hard cider, unfortunately. You'll hear about it soon enough, so I might as well tell you."

Lighthorse thought: *Maybe* she *had been drinking, maybe that explained* her *action at the door.*

Mr. Lee was saying: "I'm sorry to hear that. By the way," he added quickly, "where did you find Elmo? I hope he wasn't any place he shouldn't have been."

"Oh no," Mr. Sutton said. "I noticed him when I went to get Selma—that's my wife. She was at her first meeting with the Joy Bearers—you know the church group?"

Mrs. Lee nodded. "Minnie Arkwright is the president, I know."

"Well, your son—is it Elmo?—he was sitting in the snow on the steps of the Moravian Church. Sitting the way—well, I've had a good bit of experience judging that. So I let Selma ride home with Nelda Owens, and I brought Elmo." Mr. Sutton got to his feet, and Mrs. Lee said, "You're sure you wouldn't want another cup?"

"Oh no, no thanks," he said, placing the cup and saucer on the table. "I'll have to be getting along," he added, going to the living room and reaching for his overcoat and scarf.

"Here," Mr. Lee said, taking the coat from Lighthorse and holding it. "By the way," he added at the door, "I'll not forget this favor." He held out his hand.

"Don't mention it—and thanks to you folks for doing the laundry so promptly." Mr. Sutton stepped through the door.

A moment later there came a knock; and Mr. Sutton thrust his head back in the door and said, "You may not know it but you've got a few window peepers. I hope I didn't bring them."

"No—no, but thanks for telling me." Mr. Lee closed the door and paced back and forth. Then he pounded his fist into his palm. He went to the waterbucket that stood near the washstand in the kitchen and was on his way to the stairs when Mrs. Lee said, "Nat, you're not going to do that."

"Of course I am."

"They'll think you're dumping the chamber pot."

"So much the better!" Mr. Lee bounded up the stairs. From the bedroom above the front room there came the soft sound of a window being raised and then Mr. Lee's voice rang out, "Just a moment—I'll empty the chamber pot." There was the sound of cascading water and then a jumble of shrieks and muffled footbeats from beyond the small bay-window of the front room.

"Nat, you didn't!"

"Certainly I did."

"He sure did," Lighthorse said to Hubert, "bullseye on target!"

"I hope Minnie Arkwright is fool enough to bury her clothes," Mr. Lee added.

"Who were the others? Could you see?"

"I don't know and don't give a damn," Mr. Lee said. "I'll bet dimes to doughnuts there are at least three wiser Joy Bearers in Gnadenhutten tonight."

"What will you say if they ask you about this?" Mrs. Lee went to sit down in a rocking chair in the front room.

"I'll say every man's home is his castle and he can dump his pot when he pleases." Mr. Lee began to laugh, and Lighthorse and Hubert joined him.

A short while later, after Hank and Hubert and Light-horse had settled warm in the bed they shared, and Hessie was in her upstairs cot beside her parents' bed, Lighthorse heard his father announce: "Mary, I don't want you to stay up with these boys. I'll stay now and if I get tired I'll call one of the others."

"You know you won't call them. And you have to work tomorrow."

"I'll call them if I need them. Besides, this is my fault, somehow."

"Nat, you don't need to feel that."

"Mary, you're too good to a weak husband."

"Nonsense!"

"Don't nonsense me!" There was the sound of their feet on the stairs, possibly a little heavier than usual, and then the sound of two voices in the front bedroom. They said something about Mr. Sutton and his situation, something that by its tone spoke sympathy, and then they spoke quietly to each other as Lighthorse had heard them so often. A little later he heard his father descend the stairs to begin the vigil beside his three inebriated sons, a vigil that ended with the three sons and the father drinking black coffee at the breakfast table, the father looking the worst of the lot.

❧ 14 ❦

A five-inch snow fell throughout the night. It lay on the ground through eight days of clear cold weather, and on the ninth day, Friday, the air turned warm, and the snow grew wet and heavy and of precisely the right texture for packing a sled path. That evening, under a full moon that piled pristine white on white, Lighthorse and Nancy Sutton made their way down Walnut Street, side by side, avoiding the sled that dogged their heels. Each wore a heavy mitten on one hand—Lighthorse had borrowed his father's fleece-lined work mittens, after promising care that was now forgotten—and their ungloved hands locked together as they ran.

Where the cleared sidewalk ended in a snow-packed path and the schoolyard sloped away to what in summer was a creek of coal mine drainage, Lighthorse flung the sled ahead and Nancy leaped upon it. She kept her balance as Lighthorse leaped on behind her, his arms encircling her, his hands fighting for the clothesline pull-rope she had yanked from his grasp.

The sled, which had been running the gentle slope of the beaten path, suddenly veered right to plunge over the fifteen-foot embankment of the creek. Falling, falling toward the cushion of drifted snow in the shadow of the frozen creek bed, they locked arms and landed together. For one long moment they lay without need of speech— toboggans and mittens gone, Nancy's dark hair blown against his face, her cheek cool and apple-fragrant against his lips. Then, as Lighthorse moved to rise, Nancy caught his hand and slid it beneath her pink sweater against the warm swell of her breast, and her teeth gleamed as she nipped his cheek and ear.

Lighthorse had but dimly known such times could come, and when he began to rise, Nancy was above him, her fingers laced in his, unbelievably strong, bending him back, forcing him down as her teeth closed hard on the flesh of his exposed neck. And before he could stand erect, as he felt he must, she was gone, scrambling up the bank, uttering a strange animal cry.

"Wow!" Lighthorse exclaimed, after he gathered up the mittens and caught up with her and the sled she now pulled, "I'd sure hate to tangle with you—if I couldn't stand you."

Laughing, still trotting, she whispered, "Would you stand me?"

Then she was motioning ahead, toward the hill where the beaten path led, the towering height of Stalwart's Hill. Three rollercoaster curves, almost a quarter mile in length, formed the structure of the hill, topped by a sharp dome above the icy track being built by the many pairs of gleaming steel runners. Starting from any one of the three roller-coaster grades, sleighers could sweep across the hundred yards of flat pastureland, and upward through the opened pasture gate, across the graveled extension of Walnut Street and onward through the long hayfield that led to the playgrounds of the schools.

Now Stalwart's Hill formed a backdrop for a huge fire of dead chestnut logs, about which the sleighers stood to gain some warmth before mounting again to the upper levels to hurl themselves into space—and it was toward that fire that Nancy raced Lighthorse. They slowed to a walk as they crossed the hayfield where the most daring and highest climbing sleighers coasted to a halt. When one sled stopped at their feet, Lighthorse asked, "How's the trail, Steve?"

"Slick as cat's fur!"

"Really fast, eh?" Lighthorse said. "And look at that moon. We'll really have an evening!" He pulled Nancy against him, saying, "Steve Owens goes as high as anyone. He and Ted Biggers usually fight it out for the highest start." He waved toward the top of the towering hill.

"Do they go higher than you?"

"They always have," Lighthorse said. "You can see that some just start at the first cowpath, and others the second, and sometimes Ted and Steve work clear up to the third."

"Is that as high as anyone can go?" Nancy asked as they approached the fire.

"The hill goes higher—you'll see when we get there." Lighthorse led Nancy around the fire, exchanging a greeting here and there, wanting others to see her but not willing for her to stop to talk. "Let's go right up for a first ride. Then we'll stop and get warm." They joined the many shadows climbing, and he steered her well clear of the track down

76

which the sleds streaked. "Don't look back until I tell you," he said.

Where the first cowpath crossed the hill, he swung her around. "Now look."

"Gee, have we climbed that much?" The lights of the town lay below them like fireflies. Nearer, the huge bonfire had become grate size, and the sleighers around the fire Lilliputians.

"This is just the first slope. There are two more and then the straight-climb. What would you like?—we could ride down *together* from here."

"I'd like to climb higher."

"Well, we'll not be able to ride together, but we could take turns from the second path. Up we go!" Lighthorse yanked the sled after them.

When they stood on the relatively flat extension where the second cowpath circled the hill, Lighthorse turned her around. "Like it?" he whispered, reaching for her bare hand.

"Like it! It's wonderful! Look at the fire—no bigger than a shovelful of coals." Nancy's eyes followed the sled track. "I had no idea it was so high."

"You wait till we get to the third path!" Lighthorse dropped the sled rope. "Tell you what, let's walk up there now just to get a look."

"Aren't you going to go from up there? Look!" Nancy caught his arm. "There's someone coming from up there now." As she spoke, a black object shot down the track some twenty feet to their left.

"That's Steve—Steve Owens, the guy we spoke to down-hill," Lighthorse said. "He's got a good sled."

"Isn't yours a good sled?" Nancy looked at the sled at their feet.

"It's okay for the thing . . . the cheap thing it is, but it's not like Steve's." Lighthorse could have told precisely what the difference was, in both materials and price—price down to the last cent—but he didn't. Instead he reached down, yanked the sled into motion, and began climbing toward the third level.

They had climbed about half of the distance when Nancy asked, "Does Ted Biggers have a better sled too?"

Lighthorse said nothing.

"Lighthorse, does *he* go from up there too?"

"He goes from up there." Lighthorse's voice was on edge.

"Does he have a better sled than yours?"

"Hell yes, he's got a better sled. He's got the best goddamn sled in town. Now what of it?"

Nancy stopped, and Lighthorse turned to her. "You're getting tired?"

"No. I'm not tired at all, and I don't like for you to talk to me like that."

"Well I didn't mean anything." Lighthorse looked at her, hoping she'd see what he couldn't say. "You asked me a question—twice—and I answered."

"You didn't answer the way you should."

"Are you telling me how I should answer?"

"Of course not!" She turned, head down, and began walking away from him, then running downhill to the left.

He watched her move away, sick at heart, but in his anger willing that she should go. And then in crystal vision he saw the tragedy of his action. She had moved directly onto the sled path, and from some hundred feet above a black projectile hurtled toward her.

Without being conscious that he moved, Lighthorse dived down upon her from behind. He couldn't drag her back, but he could and did knock her clear even as he felt a stinging caress like a sharp knife drawn lengthwise across his face and ear. A thousand bees were stinging in his ears, his head, and he was aware of falling from a great height. He was falling from a height as in a dive, and his dive had carried him downhill across pasture and hayfield, across schoolhouse and town, to a black depth such as he had never known even when he was fifteen feet under water in the Tuscarawas River. The weight of space closed upon him.

≫ 15 ≪

Lighthorse lay in darkness. Only one idea came through
and that idea had no relationship to space or time, and
perhaps was less an idea than instinctive impulse: he
was dead but he could be born again.

In the filmy dark the notion came to him that this was his
first real choice in life, and it could be made independently
of all influences: church, town, school and family. Should
he choose, he would settle back into the continued comfort
of no time, or he could raise his eyelids and see whatever
of the world was his to see. Even as his mind ranged his
world in search, his body was slipping into the stream of
time. The shore slid from beneath his feet. A choice was
being made, he was already afloat. He had only to let go,
lie back, and be eternally wrapped.

A second idea stopped him, turned his toes to claws that
dug the riverbottom and held firm. By not choosing either
to live or die he was dying. And he had not been allowed

to choose. In the realization that he didn't care, didn't really care, he let the gentle water raise his body and ease him backward the step he had fought to gain. Even as he let death have its way—not choosing is choosing—he reckoned one twilight balance and another.

While he held on to life, more in stubbornness than with reason, he heard a voice that spoke no intelligible words and yet a voice which set his arms threshing, his feet climbing the sloping shore toward a face in the light of the brightest day he had known.

"Mom! Mom!" he cried aloud. Slowly the face near him came into focus in the bright light that hurt his watering eyes, and he saw that the face was quite close, all but touching his. "Hessie, Hessie," he said loudly, "where's Mom? Didn't you hear me call her? Hessie, do you hear me?"

"Mom!" Hessie called, "Mom, come here! He's awake. He just mumbled something."

Lighthorse saw his mother enter the room; and he spoke a reprimand: "You wouldn't need to run."

He closed his eyes—he was tired, exhausted—and when, minutes later, he opened them again, he had trouble formulating his questions. "Did you—Mom, did you say or do something just before I called out?"

"He didn't call out—I was listening and he just barely grunted," Hessie explained to her mother.

"I called," Lighthorse said, ignoring Hessie, "I called you but right before I called, did you say something?"

"Yes I did say something," Mrs. Lee said. "Dad and the boys are out, and I was paring potatoes in the kitchen, but I think I was talking some sort of almost nonsense to myself."

"That must've been what I heard," Lighthorse said. He

raised a finger to explore the bandages that lay like a cold pack on his head.

"I know one thing," Hessie said, "you two sure do lie. Lighthorse didn't call you; he was here in the front room and he just barely grunted. And you didn't say anything, because I'd have heard it."

"Well, you know what you know, dear." Mrs. Lee wrapped a finger in Hessie's light brown hair and gave a gentle tug.

Lighthorse slept, and when he awoke it was evening. The house was fragrant with fresh baking, and his father and Elmo were sitting beside the davenport, his father reading the front page of the paper, Elmo the sports section. From beneath his bandages Lighthorse watched a moment; they both read much too fast to be reading, and when they caught one another glancing at him, they each turned a page and went through the motions of reading again. When he had watched long enough that he felt he would have to speak or explode, Lighthorse said, "Hey, you two—what's new?"

"Well!" Mr. Lee's paper went up and out, and Elmo's collapsed against his chest. "Lighthorse, you rascal! Mary— Mary," Mr. Lee called, and the rattle of dishes ceased. "Mary, this fellow's okay again."

"He's spouting rhymes *we'll* probably die from," Elmo said.

"Good for him!" Mrs. Lee, followed by Ed and Everett, entered the room. "Do you want something for supper, Lighthorse? Do you think you could eat a bowl of potato soup?"

"You could always offer him a bowl of beans—navy beans," Ed said. He looked from Elmo to Everett expectantly and as he raised his hand to mark time, they chanted in unison:

"Beans, beans, the musical fruit,
The more you eat, the more you toot,
The more you toot, the better you feel,
So eat beans for every meal."

"You three belong in vaudeville," Mr. Lee said. "You could accompany one another on a musical toilet seat."

"All right, smart alecs," Mrs. Lee exclaimed. "I asked Lighthorse whether he wanted a bowl of potato soup."

"Didn't you fix him the oysters I brought?" Elmo asked.

"Of course I did," Mrs. Lee said, "but I want him to eat something with a little body to it."

"Oysters! Lighthorse, you lucky guy," Everett said. "The only time I ever got oyster soup was when I had my tonsil operation and couldn't eat solids."

"You should kick," Mr. Lee said casually. "I never even tasted oysters until after I was grown up and married."

"I'd rather have my tonsils out to earn mine," Elmo said.

Mrs. Lee drew a deep breath but said nothing. She looked from father to sons, and Lighthorse could feel her joy.

"*That* was the reasoning behind Dad's statement," Everett explained.

"Sure," Elmo taunted as he moved to the doorway. "Dad said that so smoothly you didn't even get it."

"Nat, did you?" Mrs. Lee picked up Hessie's geography book, walked beside him, and swung it solidly.

"Lighthorse, you'd better get up and let a wounded man lie down," Mr. Lee complained as he rubbed his buttocks.

"Nat—all of you, just quit making him laugh. You'll rip his stitches or something." Mrs. Lee came to stand above the davenport. "You really do feel better?"

"If I felt any better my stitches would be ripping," Lighthorse said. "Without beans."

83

"Straining with beans begets ripping nine times out of ten," Mr. Lee explained solemnly to Elmo. "The polite term is *flatus*, I prefer fart."

"I was a four-letter man even in high school," Elmo said.

"Nat, you're going to pay for these shenanigans."

"Did I start them?" Mr. Lee asked as he moved to the safety of the dining room.

"Yes you did. And you're egging them on, and you know it." She was smiling at Lighthorse.

"Lighthorse, you'd better believe me when I tell you you could have heard the old thunder jug rattle in this house last night," Elmo said.

"And brother, did it!" Everett said. "Nervous people, nervous people."

"There's no sense in this family," Mrs. Lee said, turning to leave the room.

"Mom," Lighthorse said, "what day is this? How long have I been here?"

"This is Sunday," Mrs. Lee said. "And if it's even a trifle holy the Lees aren't to blame."

"Aw, Mom," Elmo said, "you know we're just feeling a little good."

"The last time you boys were feeling good we had two of you stretched out on that same davenport," Mr. Lee called from the table where he had gone to begin laying out the knives and forks.

"Nat, I'm going to muzzle you if it's the last thing I do," Mrs. Lee said as she moved to him.

"Well, I guess it's a regular Sunday all right," Lighthorse said to Everett.

"No, it's not, Lighthorse," Hessie said from the doorway, "Dad bought a quart of ice cream. He never does that on a regular Sunday. Mom and I baked an angel food cake too." She was pirouetting on her left toe.

"It sure sounds like a wake instead of a recovery," Elmo said to Lighthorse.

"It's more like a birth than either."

"I don't get that, I don't get that at all."

"That's what it is," Lighthorse repeated, feeling he could claim the prerogative of being misunderstood.

"Lighthorse—Lighthorse!" Mr. Lee called from the kitchen—and it was evident he was struggling to escape a hand over his mouth. "I had your mother in my arms as you spoke that birth bit—you stopped us cold."

"Dad!" Hessie cried out, "don't forget I'm here."

"Honey child, we can live with our past," Mr. Lee said, "but our future's a gamble."

"Hessie dear, you ignore this mad man and come help Mother with the supper."

"Things don't look so good and then they sometimes straighten out," Mr. Lee announced from the kitchen.

"The governor's hitting on all seven cylinders," Everett said to Lighthorse.

"Lord save us from eight!" Elmo exclaimed.

≥ 16 ≤

The Suttons—Nancy and her mother and father—came to call on Monday evening. Mrs. Lee and Hessie had spent the weekend cleaning, dusting, shining, and polishing —and Elmo protested he did not plan to have his meagre bare-assed personal account inspected by white-gloved bank examiners. Lighthorse sensed that Elmo had gone out of his way to voice his revulsion, and that only added to his own anxiety. And when at eight o'clock Hessie announced the Suttons' Buick had slowed to a stop in front of the house, Lighthorse heard Elmo and Everett slam out the back door while Ed and Hank and Hubert made their way upstairs.

Mr. Lee, clad in his Sunday serge and white shirt, stood at the front door taking hats and coats; and Mrs. Lee, dressed in her Sunday black voile with lace bodice, led the Suttons into the front room turned hospital. Lighthorse noticed that Nancy was wearing her pink sleighing sweater and a gray skirt, and that both she and her father had come as they were, for her father's brown suit coat was worn through at the elbow. Mrs. Sutton, who lingered at the door with a critical roving eye and then crossed quickly to the chair Mr. Lee held for her, was clad in a red wool dress and a white fur jacket, the same red wool Lighthorse had seen as she shut the door in his face. And this time her jewelry was altogether different, a twisted string of pearls at her neck, and a heavy band of gold with bright gems, diamonds perhaps, on her wrist.

The niceties of the evening—cold and blowing with threat of further storm—having been settled at the door, Mr. Sutton sat down on one of the wobbly straight-backed chairs that went with the dining set, and edged it around to face Lighthorse. Nancy ignored the chair that Hessie pointed to and dropped onto the floor, leaning back against her father's legs. Nudged by Mrs. Lee, Hessie, who was regarding Mrs. Sutton with that awe she ordinarily reserved for the Christmas tree, followed Nancy's example, her back against her father's legs, even as Mrs. Sutton said, "Nancy Sutton, where *are* your manners?"

Lighthorse had been awaiting Nancy's first word—and now she said: "I'm glad Dad got Mom to come, but I would've come by myself if I'd had to."

Lighthorse smiled.

Mrs. Sutton had audibly drawn in her breath, but Mr. Sutton's quick comment stopped her second reprimand. "You can see how necessary parents are today." He winked at Mr. Lee.

"I always had a pet theory on that," Mr. Lee said.

"Nat has many pet theories; few of them are tame enough for the polite society of Gnadenhutten," Mrs. Lee explained to Mrs. Sutton.

"So far I haven't found a thimbleful of politeness or a mouse trace of society in this town. If Clarence had an inch of drive we'd be living in Philadelphia or New York this minute." Mrs. Sutton let her eyes settle momentarily on her husband as she spoke.

"Hooray for this town and the old plow horse!" Mr. Sutton said, turning to look down on Nancy and Lighthorse. "Lighthorse meet plow horse," he added.

"I've always had a pet theory on parenthood," Mr. Lee repeated. His tone said he was seeking to guide the conversation.

"Parenthood—with control—is essential, don't you think?" Mrs. Sutton announced. "I'm sure nothing is so vital to our standard of living today." Almost in the same breath she added to Mrs. Lee, "Your son had something tragic about him the night he brought my laundry, poor child."

Nancy had been looking up at her mother. She winced, and turned to Lighthorse. He shrugged and Hessie giggled. Nancy touched the crocheted bedspread, caught a tassel and twisted it around a braid of her hair. Her eyes focused on the braid as she spoke quietly to Lighthorse, asked about his head and the bandages, and then began talking about English and history assignments.

Mr. Sutton said to Mr. Lee, "I'm not sure I meant what I said about parents. Are parents really necessary?"

"I've always had a pet theory on parents," Mr. Lee put in half-heartedly.

"How do you feel about this town? Or have you been here long enough to get lost in the rut without realizing it?" Mrs. Sutton said to Mrs. Lee.

"Dear," Mr. Sutton said, "Mr. Lee has a theory."

"Well it's not much of a theory really," Mr. Lee said, glancing at his wife. "Actually it's pretty dated, but I guess it's what Mary and I try to live by."

"This is news to me," Mrs. Lee said quickly. "After all these years I'm to be informed." A smile formed along the wrinkle lines in her face.

"My theory isn't that important, I'm afraid," Mr. Lee went on. "But I do think there exists a sort of debt of the generations. I could never repay my parents all they did for me, and so I have a debt to my own children. It's not exactly a mathematical computation," he added weakly as Mrs. Sutton said, "Clarence, don't you think we should be going? It's obvious that these good people have work to do; and as you can see, the boy's perfectly all right." Lighthorse whispered to Nancy: "I'm the boy."

"Yes." Nancy folded two fingers into a spear—then gently touched his cheek.

"No." Mr. Sutton spoke without looking at his wife. "I don't think we should be going. What did you say about mathematical computation, Nat?"

"Mother, you can't go now! We just got here," Nancy said.

"Yes," Mrs. Sutton fixed her dark eyes on Nancy, "you would agree with him. Go ahead and make me suffer, the two of you. Did you ever—" her voice faltered but gathered strength, "did you ever do one single thing I wanted to do without forcing me to beg you to do it? Did you? Or you?" She had turned on Mr. Sutton. "Of course not!"

Mr. Lee looked at his wife and swallowed; his throat made a whack-whack noise, and he started to say something about coffee but Mrs. Sutton cut him off.

"What do you do—what *can* you do when you're being martyred, murdered and martyred, right in your own house? Well, what do you do? I want you to tell me."

Nancy leaned forward wrapping and unwrapping the braid of her hair, and whispered to Lighthorse: "Now you get an earful!" Mr. Sutton tugged on Nancy's free braid and silenced her.

"Selma," he said, "you must remember that the Lees aren't really concerned about our domestic circumstances."

"How many *children* do you have?" Mrs. Sutton said to Mrs. Lee.

"We have five other sons," Mrs. Lee said. "Lighthorse is our youngest."

"Lighthorse," Mr. Sutton began, "Lighthorse we . . ."

"Well, I wish to God Clarence had married you instead of me. All he has talked since Nancy Lee was born is children, children, children, till I feel like an incompetent incubator. I wish to God he had married you."

Mrs. Lee looked at Mr. Lee, but he was shaking his head.

"Now Selma," Mr. Sutton said, "we're here to visit Lighthorse."

"I do like your nickname," Mrs. Sutton said, as she smiled and turned to Lighthorse.

"It's from American history," Mr. Sutton said. "Lighthorse, you tell us who. . ."

"Sure," Lighthorse said, making a deprecating mouth to Nancy. "The name's from Lighthorse Harry Lee of the American Revolution, the father of Robert E. Lee. It's sort of old-timey and corny, but because I inherited Nat Lee for a poppa I'm stuck with it, unless I pull my own American Revolution."

"Yes," Mrs. Sutton said, "and my mother's people were here before that revolution occurred, and what the hell good did it do them—or me? Well, Clarence"—she stood up—"I'm going, whether you are or not." Suddenly she stretched her arms wide and pressed her fists against her forehead, then said calmly: "On second thought, I'll just walk home. Why speak of your forebears if you lack the courage to follow them."

"Now Selma, that's not necessary." Mr. Sutton got to his feet. "There's snow on the ground and you aren't dressed for walking."

"Yes, but I want to. I've decided. You make him let me," Mrs. Sutton had turned to Mrs. Lee.

"Really, I . . ." Mrs. Lee lifted her hands.

"Aw, let her go, Dad," Nancy said. "She's got her boots on and it's just a dozen or so blocks straight ahead." She looked at Lighthorse as if ready to laugh, but he sensed tears were an equal probability. She leaned closer to him and said he was being missed at school—by Miss Tillotson and others who would remain nameless.

Mrs. Sutton moved to the door and Mr. Lee handed out her jacket but stood before her, his hand on the knob.

"We'll all go; you've been very kind," Mr. Sutton said to Mrs. Lee.

"I'm walking, Clarence," Mrs. Sutton said and motioned for Mr. Lee to get out of her way. Mr. Lee looked at Mr. Sutton, who wasn't yet into his coat.

Mr. Lee opened the door to show the condition of the night to Mrs. Sutton. "It's blustery, bleak, and cold as blazes," he said.

"I like that," Mrs. Sutton said. "Such a night I understand."

Even while whispering with Nancy, Lighthorse could sense that his father was plainly rattled, as he said: "Mary, call one of the boys. Is Elmo upstairs, he can hold a flashlight. Elmo, ho, Elmo!"

"He's out," Hessie said. "He and Everett went out before the Suttons came. Elmo said he wasn't getting stuck. . ."

"Never mind, Hessie!" Mrs. Lee exclaimed. "Never mind!"

"Selma, do you have to walk?" Mr. Sutton said to his wife. "You've already shown your mettle."

"I want to, and I will."

"Get one of the others—Hank or Ed," Mr. Lee motioned for Mrs. Lee to detain Mrs. Sutton as he went to the stairs.

"Edward!" he called from the foot of the stairs.

"What? Who?"

"Edward!"

"Yes."

"You come hold a flashlight for Mrs. Sutton."

Ed Lee appeared at the top of the stairs, his face paled with sleep, his hair rumpled, his eyes adjusting to the light.

"You wanted me?"

"You're to get into your jacket and walk Mrs. Sutton home," Mr. Lee said.

"What the deuce—" He motioned toward Mr. Sutton.

"Never mind. You just get into your jacket."

"Come along, Edward," Mrs. Lee said.

Mrs. Sutton pushed Mrs. Lee's arm aside and walked out into the night.

Nancy said to Lighthorse: "There she goes, I knew she would!" Lighthorse nodded; he had been thinking how closely Nancy resembled her mother.

A look of "why-me" clouding his face, Ed Lee thundered downstairs, tucking in his shirttail as he came. He paused to pull on his jacket and cap; Mr. Lee thrust a feebly glowing two-cell flashlight into his hand and he stumbled after Mrs. Sutton.

Mr. Sutton watched them from the porch and then returned to stand above the sofa on which Lighthorse lay.

"Nancy and I wanted a great deal to visit you, Lighthorse," Mr. Sutton said. "I see you've already done your share of visiting," he said to Nancy, who blushed. "Could you tell us what you talked about—just generally?" he asked with a roguish expression.

"Mostly school and books," Hessie put in. "I listened."

"No mention of this matter you and I discussed, eh, Nancy?" Mr. Sutton said.

Nancy shook her head.

"They talked about how much bandage is around his head," Hessie said, "and whether clamps or stitches hurt most."

"Mr. Lee," Mr. Sutton said, "I don't know whether Lighthorse told you what happened the night of the accident?"

"He did," Mr. Lee said. "He slipped and fell in front of Ted Biggers' sled."

"Well, Nancy's version is slightly different. Nancy, here's your chance. Speak up."

Her eyes directly ahead, on the tip of her braid in her hand, Nancy said, "He jumped in front of the sled just to push me out of the way. He kept me from being hit—crippled or killed, maybe."

Lighthorse had an impulse to pass his hand in front of Nancy's eyes, anything to cause her to look at him.

"Did you, Son?" Mr. Lee asked.

"Forget the heroics!" Lighthorse said. "You see"—he stopped and felt for words, but finding none really satisfactory, went on—"I caused the whole crappy thing: Nancy's getting in front. . ."

"Lighthorse!" Nancy stopped him.

"I'm going to tell the whole thing."

"No, but you're not."

Mr. Sutton and Mr. Lee matched looks.

"Oh yes I am."

"You are not!" Nancy was on her feet. "Mr. Lee, if he says one word more you make him tell the whole thing—understand the whole thing—since he promised that." She looked down on Lighthorse.

A look of incredulity, and Lighthorse murmured, "Well, we'll not replay that broken record."

"That's better," Nancy said.

"I don't think this makes much sense," Hessie said to Mr. Sutton.

"Neither do I," Mr. Sutton said, "but I sort of like it."

"Is there something wrong with your wife too?" Hessie asked.

Mr. Sutton's nervous laughter prevented whatever correction Mr. and Mrs. Lee might have offered.

Later, when Mr. Sutton and Nancy had gone and the boys had returned and gone to their room and Mrs. Lee and Hessie had gone to bed, Mr. Lee left the kitchen to stand beside the davenport. "Lighthorse?"

"Yes."

"Son, I don't want to be a spying spider, but I want to ask you one question."

"Okay."

"Son, you and that Nancy girl—she's a very nice girl, but you haven't been going off the deep end—I mean you haven't been . . . going too far? She spoke so cryptically and shut you up so quickly here tonight."

Lighthorse smothered the impulse to laugh. "We went all the way to Stalwart's Hill, Dad. It was a moonlight night and we fell off the path into a snowdrift, but we got out again. We had a little quarrel and she walked in front of a sled but didn't get hurt, and—"

"And what?"

"That's everything. I've told you everything—just as she dared me to do." Lighthorse laughed now, at himself.

"Well, I couldn't think there was anything else," Mr. Lee said. "You've got the makings, Lighthorse."

"Maybe I'd better take up smoking, eh?"

"All right, Long Pants, there are makings much more

important than those for roll-your-own cigarettes. And don't let me catch you taking up smoking." Mr. Lee lowered his voice: "Lighthorse, you do understand about this other—this sexual intercourse between man and woman? You understand what I explained to you and Hank and Hubert when we were all going swimming that time?"

"You mean that discourse on intercourse, of course?"

"Okay, Mister!" Mr. Lee laughed. "Well, I forget exactly what I did say about it, but I want to repeat one thing. With the right woman that exchange is one of the fine things of your life. It's worth waiting for, and our society being organized around the family the way it is—and it still is, even in Philadelphia or New York, poor woman—there's good sense to waiting, not waiting childishly but waiting because only in marriage can the exchange be entirely free and open, and as often as both husband and wife might like." Mr. Lee paused, "Does that make sense or am I just mouthing words?"

"Mom always says you make more sense than dollars. I agree."

"Yes. Well, there was so damned much self-esteem shown by several persons here tonight, I feel a little semi-precious myself."

"*She* sure did go on," Lighthorse said. "Dad—you don't think that would affect Nancy? I mean she's not likely to end up like her mother, is she?"

"Well, it's bound to affect her but not necessarily the way you mean. She'll probably outgrow her ills."

"When I went to her house that night I was feeling pretty sick because I didn't have her chances. And now all I want to do is someday make sure she has mine."

"That's a thought for the self-esteem bin too," Mr. Lee said.

"I mean it."

"Then *un*mean it—and that reminds me, Elmo wanted me to tell you one thing."

"He couldn't tell me himself?"

"He could, but he didn't want to. He didn't want you to misunderstand, and he didn't want to hurt you either."

"What's that?"

"Elmo wants you not to make up your mind on any girl— even such a nice girl as Nancy Sutton—until you've made a fair start in college. Maybe I'm not stating that too subtly, but he means well by you, Lighthorse."

"I know he does." There was a silence and Lighthorse became aware of the alarm clock ticking on the table. He realized his father had had the alarm clock and white enameled chamber pot in hand, en route to bed—that time was passing, and his father had to get up at 5:30 a.m. to walk to work. "Elmo'd give me the patches off his pants."

"Sure he would. Elmo's a good one—a really good one —if he just didn't have such lousy taste in literature. Oh well, it'd be a stale world if we had seven little Nathaniel P. Lees running around."

"Dad, you're talking in your sleep—there are only six of us boys."

"Count your old pop, Son." He laid a fist on Lighthorse's ribs, took up the alarm clock and the chamber pot, and called "Goodnight" from the stairs.

❧ 17 ❦

Lighthorse found the three-week convalescence ordered by Doctor Spears too long, despite a second visit by Nancy Sutton and her father and two visits by Miss Tillotson. The house could not hold him once the bandages were removed from his head. Every sunny afternoon he pulled on Elmo's heavy blue turtleneck sweater and worn hunting boots, and tramped down bleak streets and through snowy pasture fields and corn fields to the river's edge opposite the great shale bluff above the town, there to follow the river downstream as it held the town in its deep-crooked arm.

He walked to reconfirm earth and sky and river, the world from which his three-day death had snatched him. And as he probed nature he read more completely each story: the tale told by fox tracks, two sets of which ran together upwind, separated for a hundred feet, and then closed on what was now only an ominous red blotch to which clung bits of rabbit down. Or a similar tale of sudden death, this time from the sky, where a red-shouldered hawk had dived to end a second rabbit's life. Snow delicately sculpted by wings said here fell the fluff cloud that blotted the plunging rabbit's life, but nothing recorded how sharp the talons, how deep the thrust, yet Lighthorse knew and trembled for the striker and the one struck down.

On a bright Friday noon as he started out to lope down Walnut Street toward the railroad tracks that he might walk the tracks eastward and then cross open fields to the river and follow it downstream to the cemetery, he was stopped short by his own name. "Lighthorse! Lighthorse, wait for me."

Lighthorse turned in the direction of the school. Excited faces above up-and-down pumping arms and legs announced the noon outpour—the homeward rush to lunch.

"Lighthorse," Nancy called, "where you going? Mind if I go too?"

"I'm going right past your house, I'll walk you home."

"You're really okay again?" Nancy motioned toward the thin scab above his right ear.

"Sure. I'm starting to school on Monday."

"But where are you going now?"

"I'm taking a little walk along the river. Just for fun. I've even got a lunch here." He shook the potato sack in his left hand. "Mom's not feeling well, so last night Hessie packed her own lunch to take to school and this one for me. I'd just as soon eat out on the riverbank; I can go farther—walk and eat at the same time."

"Why do you need to go farther—I don't even know where you're going."

"I'm going to follow the river. Don't you ever listen?"

"Would you mind if I came along?"

"You couldn't. You've got school and your mother wouldn't want you. . ."

"She'll not care. She's out of this world these days." Nancy rocked her head back and forth.

"That's too bad."

"Oh, I don't know. It's not too bad because now I can go with you."

"Did I ask you?" His tone betrayed his hope. "You've still got to go to school."

"But I'll not go. I'll just stay away. Do I have to stick my head under a sled so I can get half a day off? I'll just stay away. I'll be your nurse or something."

"I'd prefer the something."

"Yes?" Her eyes, capable of jetting fire, grew tender and dark as she traced the scar above his ear.

"Your mouth is open—do you know?"

"Damn you."

"I like it—but it was open, Pink Tongue."

"Can I go?" She stepped back.

"You sure you want to?"

"Of course, silly. I'm going to ask just once more. Can I?"

"How do I know. I'm not your keeper." He smiled.

"Well why didn't you say so?"

When they came to the Sutton house, Nancy pretended she would turn in. She did turn in—to pick up an apple switch that stuck up like a snare trap in the snow—and cut a neat scissor-legged circle out again to join Lighthorse, who kept walking straight ahead. "I could pack a lunch to take along."

"That's not necessary." Lighthorse hefted the potato sack. "If I know Hessie, she's packed a banquet."

"What a day!" Nancy motioned to the sky and sun, and kicked a puff of powder snow into the air and swung the apple switch through it. Lighthorse grabbed at his forehead, rubbed it with the flat of his hand.

"Gee, did I hit you?"

"No, a snake bit me. Here, give me it!" He took the switch and tamped it upright in the snow. "People will know that Adam and Eve have been here—and gone."

"I would have broken it in two."

He said, "It'll grow and be our winter apple tree. Come on, let's run." They ran and then they walked; and they ran again when they began to follow the railroad tracks, for he wanted them to get entirely off the road-bed before a train came, blowing cinders and soot upon them. But they didn't get to the turn-off point before a passenger train bore down upon them, and rather than walk on facing the whirling wheels, terrible in thrust and power at that closeness, Lighthorse spun her around and they stood with their backs to the pelting bits of cinder.

"There's something awful about a train," Nancy said. "And this is the one week I didn't braid my hair." She bent forward tossing her hair over her face, shaking the cinders from it. Lighthorse preferred her hair loose, like the mane of a running filly, but he said nothing as she flipped her head back and tucked the resplendent mass beneath her scarf. "When you're riding in a coach, trains are all right, but down here—on wheel level—they're terrible."

"I've thought that too. I never told Hank or Hube or even Elmo, but I've always been afraid of trains."

"I'm not afraid, just disappointed. I guess they're like everything else, kind of a compromise."

"I've thought that too—I repeat myself." Lighthorse laughed. "Absolutes are for martyrs, compromises for man. You may not like it but you accept it."

"I like the word compromise—Missouri Compromise. Miss Tillotson discussed *it* this morning."

As they descended the cinder bank to cross the open

cornfield that ended at the riverbank, Lighthorse said: "Then maybe it's just as bad as it sounds. We buy a little time with a compromise, and are compromised. Is that our bargain?"

"So what if we get a little dirt in the bargain?" Again Nancy loosened her scarf, and flipped her hair forward and back as she walked. "It comes out."

Lighthorse motioned to the coal soot which had painted dark clouds across the snow field downwind from the track. "Way out. Compromise and be compromised, get a lot of unforeseen dirt in the exchange."

"Lighthorse, you don't think *your* mom and *your* dad made a bad bargain?"

"Not really."

"Mine did," Nancy said, "and I know how they continue —out of selfishness. Mother runs up and down in a bleary little world, imagining that she's the last person God made before He got careless."

"That's a pretty tough thing to say."

"It's the truth though. Sometimes"—she turned to Lighthorse—"sometimes I'd like to grab the truth like a big sword and run around chopping off the heads of those that need it. You'd find lots of deadbeats at the end of my trip."

"Now who's kidding?"

"I am not! I promise you one thing." Blood rose to tint her neck and cheeks. "If ever I turn out like my mother I promise you one thing: I won't even need a big sword. I'll grab the truth—and it'll be big enough." She pointed toward the flash of sun on water directly ahead. "I've never been afraid of water."

"I wish you wouldn't say that, or think it—ever." Lighthorse was about to tell of his own recent struggle in which the river had threatened to overwhelm him, but decided not to. He changed the subject: "What say, let's build a fire and eat some lunch? Here's an ideal spot for a fire, everything but applewood." He motioned toward a fallen sycamore tree which was still alive and held waist high by a single root. "We'll sit here and I'll start a fire right there." He brushed snow off the tree, scraped the ground clear in front of it, and began collecting the dry twigs and leaves scattered under it. In no time he had a foot-high pile.

"You can unpack the lunch, Pink Tongue." He nodded toward the sack and dropped down on hands and knees to light the fire. The fire caught slowly, one leaf and then another; he blew the sparks to life and judiciously added match-, then pencil-size sticks, and when at last he got to his feet the tepee of inch-thick branches was sending out a plume of smoke and a clean woodsy scent.

"Well, how about lunch?"

Nancy lounged against the sycamore, her attention on the ripple of water and sun on water. "You look."

"Now if Hessie pulled a trick—" Lighthorse opened the sack. "Wouldn't you know it!" He lifted out the dirty jumble that had been two peanut butter sandwiches, a piece of chocolate cake, and an apple. The bread and the cake were coated with dirt that had clung to the potatoes the sack had once contained.

"Hessie didn't empty the sack; she didn't even wrap the sandwiches or cake. Here I was bragging about the food we'd have, and now we've got a real compromise."

"Don't say that, please. One meal more or less won't hurt me." Nancy smiled. "Here's my pink tongue, take a bite."

Lighthorse began to polish the apple on his shirt. "I doubt that *it's* edible." He held it out.

Nancy took the apple, sank her teeth into it, and turned

away, chewing. "It's real good. Here, taste it. Right here." She forced the apple on him, forced him to bite where her teeth had been. He bit and chewed, and found a morsel of dry rot in his mouth. He removed it and turned to warn her, but he had evidently got all the rot, for she continued nibbling daintily, gradually working round and round the core to the very seeds themselves.

He said, "I just remembered something—I'll be right back." He crossed the thin border of woods and scuffed in the snow in the field. In a short while he returned with an armload of what appeared to be mud balls.

"And you thought the apple wasn't edible. You and Hessie!"

"You just wait." With his knife Lighthorse was laying back the dirt to reveal a solid white center. "Taste that."

She took up the pearly white substance and touched it with her tongue.

"Taste and see." He prepared another and another, placing them in a row on the tree limb. "Winter rabbit food."

"Turnips?"

"Right! Turnips that leave you weak and drowsy, but they'll also fill your stomach." He took a man-sized bite.

"I feel a pleasant rabbitness coming on." Nancy sat down and stretched out on her coat in a pile of leaves she had pulled together while Lighthorse collected the turnips.

Lighthorse dropped down beside her, his body cushioned by hers. He said, "You're soft enough to be a rabbit—and wild enough." He laid a finger and then his hand in her loosened hair, and worked it through to caress her ear.

"I'd like to hear a marvelous story—if I'm a rabbit, I must have hungry ears. Tell me a story, a marvelous story."

"Can it be just a little odd?"

"Is it?"

"To some people it would be."

"You tell me and let me judge." Nancy turned a fibrous turnip core, inspected it, nibbled—and then tossed the core into the fiery heart of flames.

Lighthorse got to his knees, laid several small logs on the fire, then settled back against her.

"Well, it's a story old Clem Philips, who used to take care of the cemetery, told to me once. He's dead now, so you and I will be the only ones to know it. It really took place too. Someday I'll show you exactly where. In fact we'll walk there yet today—afterwhile. Now this Indian maiden had a pink tongue and she was the most beautiful. . ."

⊱ 18 ⊰

Part of the pleasure of studying with Miss Tillotson came from her thorough grasp of U. S. history. Without resorting to jingoism, she made the subject fun, and she was always ready to take advantage of the least turn of student interest, be it by question or comment. And yet just two weeks after Lighthorse returned to class, she was hardly prepared for the sudden liking Ted Biggers showed for local Ohio history. The class had passed well beyond the Revolutionary period and its aftermath, and was dealing with President Polk's scheming efforts to extend the nation westward, when Ted Biggers raised his hand to ask his question.

"Miss Tillotson"—Ted Biggers said, in the tone of one who has just discovered that even a history course might make sense on occasion—"Miss Tillotson, would it be all right for me to ask a question about our own local history before we begin discussing today's assignment?"

"Why certainly, Ted," Miss Tillotson said, glancing quickly at Lighthorse to alert him to Ted's reformation.

"Well, this has to do with local matters, our own history of Gnadenhutten," Ted Biggers said. "My question might even be called one of great local importance—could I ask it?"

"Surely," Miss Tillotson said, a trifle perturbed that Ted Biggers who had seldom asked or answered a question all year had suddenly become so much a scholar that he desired the attention of every single member of the class.

Ted Biggers turned so his eyes came to rest on Lighthorse. "Miss Tillotson, is there not one important portion of Gnadenhutten history—the Indian history—which we failed to discuss?"

"Why—I don't know." Miss Tillotson's mind flashed back. She recalled clearly having discussed the Moravian missionary David Zeisberger's Christianizing and settling the Delaware Indians in the spring of 1772, the gory details of Colonel Williamson's Pennsylvania militia perpetrating the Gnadenhutten massacre of 1782, and the re-establishment of the town by the Moravian missionary John E. Heckewelder in 1798—the entire story of the tragedy and the town as related in Howell's *History of Ohio* and Martin's *Tents of Grace: The Story of Gnadenhutten*.

"You didn't tell us the story of the Indian maiden, the beautiful Indian maiden and her lover," Ted Biggers said, his eyes continuing to rest on the reddening face of Lighthorse, who had glanced at Nancy Sutton and now stared at his hands, which slowly meshed and locked before him on his desk.

"Why, I don't believe I have ever heard that story. Would you mind telling it to us, Ted?"

"I'd sure like to!" Ted Biggers exclaimed, his victory complete. "But I've been told that Lighthorse intends to make a search, a private search for the mythical maiden, and I wouldn't want to let any of his personal secrets out of the bag." He added amid the class uproar: "I understand the maid's name is Pink Tongue."

Miss Tillotson had trouble restoring order, and when she had partially succeeded, Lighthorse got to his feet and walked from the room without shifting his stare from dead ahead. This caused the uproar to begin again, especially when Nancy Sutton leaped to her feet and ran after him, and Miss Tillotson herself rushed after the two of them. Miss Tillotson got the door to the hallway open just in time to allow the class to overhear Lighthorse shout: "You could tell that to him? You're a damned fool and I'm another."

≥ 19 ≤

After he left the schoolhouse, Lighthorse had no place to go. Moving against a bitter wind, he dragged himself home without being aware he was doing so; and once he arrived home, he found the house deserted, cold and cheerless. He left the house, crossed Walnut Street and the vacant lot beside old Miss Hempstead's house and was soon walking through Charley Baumgartner's several pastures and alfalfa fields in the direction of the giant fingers that were the smokestacks of the Biggers' Clay Plant, where Elmo now worked. Within a few minutes he was circling the countless tiers of pipes, the scrap and culls and seconds lying like spilled macaroni outermost in the yard, and next the neat tiers of firsts of the smaller pipes, then the twenty-fours and thirty-sixes in orderly row after row. He crossed from the ash yard to the kilns themselves, the unfired kilns like snow-covered igloos, the fired kilns like steaming jungle houses. He passed several workmen wheeling loads of four-inch pipe and stopped only long enough to ask if Elmo was firing or loading, and then went from one red-eyed kiln to another.

When he came upon Elmo—his powerful arms and neck bared, back muscles rising in ridges beneath the sweat-stained undershirt as he shoveled coal into the gaping red maw before him—Lighthorse held back and felt guilty that he had come. After the cleanliness and brightness of the schoolroom, this was too much; and Lighthorse turned to go, but Elmo saw him.

"Hey Lighthorse! Hey!" Elmo sent the shovel clattering and came toward him.

Lighthorse returned a weak "Hi Elmo!"

"What's up? Something at home—Mom or Dad?"

"No, I just walked away from school." Lighthorse looked around but there was no one near; Elmo and he stood as if in hell, amid the acrid sulfur fumes and whirling smoke.

"Can you—can you take a little time to talk now—you won't get fired or anything?"

"Of course not. Sewer pipes are sewer pipes, and laborers are sometimes human beings. If I did get fired, it'd probably be the best thing that could happen; I might get a job where I could use half a brain. That's my Wobbly speech for this morning. Tell me, did you have some trouble with Nosey Spiker or Granny Tillotson?"

"Nothing like that." Every second that passed, Lighthorse felt worse, knowing he was keeping Elmo from his work, and when Elmo shivered slightly, he said, "Let's go near the fire—where you'll be warm."

At the kiln fire, Elmo pulled on his worn leather gloves, picked up his eight-foot-long heavy iron poker, and began pulling huge clinkers out of the fire. As he worked he said, "Here comes old Bonehead Hudson, the yard boss. He's an uncommissioned general—jackass—so I'll have to pretend to be busy. You go ahead and talk."

"Well," Lighthorse began, "there isn't much to say except that Ted Biggers made a fool out of me."

"Ted Biggers again, eh? You know you could whip him if you'd really make up your mind to it."

"For god's sake, I can't even fight him. Not about this. I'm to blame more than he is. I told that crazy Nancy Sutton a story old Clem Philips once told me . . . and. . ."

"As you were saying?" Elmo concentrated on whacking a particularly stubborn clinker, and when it was broken in two, expertly flipped it out to reveal the live red coals beneath.

"I told her a legend old Clem Philips told me. I guess maybe I bragged a little too, but at least it was all to be between us—now she's told Ted Biggers."

"You had a secret." Elmo pursed his lips and beat at another clinker, knocked it free. "You politely shared your little secret with this Nancy Whosit?"

"More or less."

"Well, Lighthorse old boy, you are slowly becoming wise to the ways of animal and man. They're substantially the same." Elmo turned, grinned, tossed his poker aside, and grabbed up a scoop shovel and began heaving coal onto the bank of red.

"Well, I walked out of class after Ted Biggers made a damned fool out of me. I walked out and I don't think I'll go back."

"You're just done with education?" Elmo stopped shoveling, folded his glove and kissed it goodbye. "All done?"

"I don't see how I could go back."

"Bullshit!" Elmo straightened and pulled his damp undershirt away from his chest and then rubbed his hand across the small of his back. "If I were where I wanted to be, do you think I'd be shoveling coal or rodding out clinkers like a lost soul? You're damned right I wouldn't. I'd be in a college classroom or in a library or art gallery, and it wouldn't matter one iota which it was."

"I don't think I. . ." Lighthorse felt tears fill his eyes.

Elmo looked away. "Lighthorse, you never think you can do half of what you can do. I once didn't think I could perform manual labor. Dad told me to try it—I did and I can do just about as well as the next man."

"I don't like. . ."

"For God's sake, Lighthorse, do you think I like this? If I could do it—if Mom and Dad didn't need every damned cent I earn to keep food in our stomachs and clothes on our backs, I'd take old Bonehead's shovel and shove it down his gourdy throat. No little stinking fear of a bunch of half-baked school kids would cause me to toss away my chance to be something."

"You think I ought to go back?"

"Lighthorse, you and I have always got along pretty well, but if you don't get yourself back to that school in time for your next class, I'll just tell old Bonehead to take his damned shovel—and his job. I'll tell him I'm sorry as hell, but I've got to see that the one guy from our family who's going to college gets there even if I have to ram this poker up his ass and march him there. Get me?"

Elmo was grinning as he swung the poker, and so was Lighthorse as he avoided it. "Keep your tool to yourself," he exclaimed. "I get you."

"This poker'd make a mighty good weapon." Again Elmo playfully lunged at Lighthorse, waving the poker at his neck, and then thrusting it like a spear. "It might even do for a guy or a girl—Ted Biggers or Nancy Whosit."

"I get the general notion." Lighthorse kicked at a loose brick, sent it careening across the paved area surrounding the kiln. He walked with Elmo to the next fire and said, "Well, old bull. I suppose I'd better be going."

"Maybe so. By the way," Elmo beckoned Lighthorse back, "if you ever have another secret, I can tell you how to keep it. The way I keep my poetry on this job—and keep from going batty too."

"How?"

"I repeat it to myself—as often as I like. Try it." Elmo laughed and waved Lighthorse away, and when Lighthorse looked back from the edge of the yard, the powerful back and shoulders were bent above the flames.

PART THREE
1 9 3 6

ᕗ 20 ᕘ

I t is not easy to avoid a person for any great length of
time in a town with a published population of 870, a
figure said to include even the dogs and cats of Gnadenhutten, just to make sure that the village grew statistically,
but Lighthorse succeeded amazingly well for more than a
year. During that time he walked the same streets, attended
the same classes, took part in many of the same activities,
and associated with the same friends as Nancy Sutton, but
he had not spoken to her between the time she pursued him
in the hall and the bright June day she came to pick strawberries on Hans Baumholtz's truck farm, which lay on both
sides of the Pennsylvania Railroad track some two miles east
of Gnadenhutten.

First, Hank and then Hubert and finally Lighthorse had
become the acknowledged number-one picker in the Baumholtz strawberry patch, just as the three of them had replaced Elmo and Everett and Ed on the truck farm, and
even though for two summers Lighthorse had been a regular

hand working by the day, getting $1.00 for 10 hours' labor, Hans Baumholtz permitted him to pick strawberries at the going rate of 1½ cents per quart each morning during the season. Lighthorse was doubly glad to work at piecework wages, for with almost no effort he could earn more than his usual fifty cents for the half day. On many mornings he could pick upwards of one hundred quarts so that his total wage more than doubled for the day. And not only was he permitted—and expected—to earn extra money, but he was expected to help Hank and Hubert supervise the inexperienced pickers, inspect their rows and berries, and make sure that the berries ready for picking were picked and that all the berries picked came up to Hans Baumholtz's standards, which enabled him to get a premium price on the highly competitive Pittsburgh market to which the berries were trucked daily.

Now, in the slant light of sunrise, Lighthorse crouched beside the dewy, green row, aware of the earthy odor of wet straw and new berry baskets, aware that he was on test, that he had a certain honor to uphold as the number-one picker in the patch—and disturbed by a high-piled mound of raven braids that moved up and down, ahead and several rows to his right. His own shirt sleeves were rolled down for warmth and he told himself, inasmuch as he was willing to tell himself anything about the other picker in the patch —who was suddenly *the* other picker despite her thirty-two co-workers—that he was mainly concerned about her learning the work. How could the other picker keep her bare olive-tan arms from shaking with the morning chill? Or—a second thought—how could the other picker moving along the row with such grace and speed possibly be getting all the berries that hid among the frosty green leaves?

He was about to rise to answer his second question when the other picker got to her feet: elbows betrayed her motion and then the sharp rise of her trim waist, the indrawn breath that drew the loose shirt tight against her breasts. And slightly off balance, one arm straight, the other at an angle, she marched toward the mid-field tally shed bearing an eight-quart carrier brimming with choice red berries.

"Wowie!" Lighthorse murmured as he counted three empties and one half-filled basket in the carrier at his side. It took him a moment to recall that he was the fastest picker in the patch, and then he hunched forward, hands knocking spray off dew-laden plants in a frantic search for berries.

When he walked past her, carrying his eight quarts, he noticed that she already had three quarts filled in her second carrier, and then for no reason at all he was curt with pleasant, talkative Mrs. Baumholtz who tallied the berries. He was impatient as with water-bleached hands he sorted eight new baskets from the five-hundred-basket carton they were shipped in. And he hurried to return to the thin string of gold straw across the green row which showed where he had left off picking. It was chilly enough that a person should run, he told himself, but he was honest enough to add that the heaped baskets in the other picker's carrier made speed advisable if he were going to remain the number-one berry picker in the Baumholtz patch.

Later, as the sun rose and fully dried the berries, he was lost in the race the way he became lost in concentration during a test at school, but now it was his hands that moved automatically, roving in deceptively effortless certainty. And where his relative standing with competitors was not known during a test, here his relative standing was known, and with his last carrier the tally sheet showed:

NANCY SUTTON	64 quarts
LIGHTHORSE LEE	56 quarts

Still later, when he came on a row that lay beside the main irrigating hose, a row abundant with nests of luscious red berries the size of golf balls, he saw the numbers read:

NANCY SUTTON	96 quarts
LIGHTHORSE LEE	96 quarts

But she was a minute ahead of him in picking up new berry boxes and returning to the field. By now Hans Baumholtz himself had come into the patch and informed the other pickers that this was the race they had been waiting for, that Lighthorse Lee was being challenged, being whipped.

Lighthorse heard sufficient of the gravel-voiced comment to realize the meaning of defeat should he be defeated now. On his last trip to the tally shed he had seen Hank and Hubert grinning as they loaded the twenty-four-quart crates of berries into the tarpaulin-covered truck, and even though he had only seen them from the corner of his eye, he was stung by their snickers.

Faster—new power to his fingers and arms, the dull ache in his back shut from his senses by will power—faster he sent his fingers unlacing the berries to send them flowing into what seemed to be eight hungry quart baskets until the baskets overflowed and he could set off at a fast walk— pride kept it that—to the tally shed. And inside the tally shed the sheet showed:

NANCY SUTTON	120
LIGHTHORSE LEE	120

Later the sun burned down, his throat parched, and his sleeves became a hindrance on his arms, but he had no time to stop for a drink or to remove his shirt. Everywhere were green leaves to turn, red berries to snap off and toss into quart baskets that seemed to hold gallons, and what bothered him most, as his own movements became erratic, was that the white shirt which was only a blur in the corner of his eye did not alter in the least its rhythmic movement down the green row and from green row to tally shed and tally shed back to another green row.

Much later—time was forever now—he saw two figures in the book:

NANCY SUTTON	160
LIGHTHORSE LEE	160

More berries than he had ever picked in a morning! But the other picker had picked an equal number, and the wonder of her achievement her first day in a berry patch overwhelmed him. There was something appropriate too when he looked up and discovered that he was on the last row of the patch, and that the other picker was moving toward him from the opposite end, using a rabbity hop to match his own, moving with one gray-slacked leg folded beneath her, moving in a beautiful rhythm that had already etched itself in his brain.

When they met at last she said, "Hi!" and he said, "Tell me one thing: how *do* you do it?"

She laughed. "By instinct, silly. Like the snake, I'm closer to the earth."

Their hands were hurtling in the lightning snatches toward the same pocket of gleaming berries.

"But *how?*"

She laughed, and he sensed that the green fields and gold straw echoed her. "I come from a long line of berry pickers

—on my mother's side." Her olive hand brushed red upon his, thrust it full to overflowing, and when they got up to walk side by side across the green rows to the tally shed, each carried seven quarts of berries.

≥ 21 ≤

That sunny morning in the strawberry patch opened to a scarlet summer. Throughout the summer Lighthorse worked each day in the fields planted to asparagus and cucumbers and sweet corn and melons, worked at break-neck speed to earn time with Nancy. There were the long lazy hours spent in the Sutton or Lee houses, or wandering the hills—even the steep face of Stalwart's Hill and the sharp crags of Stony Bluff across the river to the northwest offered no obstacles to their feet. There were the evenings spent along the river; sometimes in the swimming pool attended by all townspeople, male and female, young and old, or more often in their private river pool with fine sand beach, a half-mile downstream from the village pool. This second pool had been the site of a gravel pit and its depths were carved treacherously irregular and deep by the huge gravel crane that scooped up the sand for the beach, but they made it their own retreat as they moved with matched prowess in the water.

Now that all was right between them there seemed no reason to be more than sympathetically kind when Mrs. Sutton returned from the sanitarium to which she had been taken in February. Nancy and Lighthorse viewed her presence as an external circumstance like the weather, even though Nancy dutifully spent less time with him and more with her mother, who seemed to show promise of recovery.

In the Lee household the shared life always changed considerably once the elements relented, once the great cast-iron coal stove—and Mrs. Lee beside it—no longer drew the family together. Even bathing became less an intimate family affair, since the same water no longer had to be used by at least two bathers as was necessary during the winter, and no longer could Hessie or Lighthorse, by age and custom the last bathers, complain of being left with ten gallons of silt and one of water. Now the huge oaken tubs were moved to the enclosed back porch, and anyone who preferred to be extra clean—cleaner than one could get with a cake of soap in the Tuscarawas River—was free to pump water from the cistern and lather himself as long as he liked. And the summer work that took Hank and Hubert and Lighthorse to the Baumholtz truck farm was less of a bond than it seemed, because Hank regularly drove on the overnight trips to Pittsburgh with a load of asparagus and sweet corn or melons and Hubert operated a tractor, while Lighthorse drove the pick-up truck and continued to perform manual labor. Then too, Elmo gave up his sewer pipe job and he and Ed went off to Pittsburgh, hoping to get work in the steel mills. Even Everett spent his free time on weekend jaunts to Pittsburgh, to visit a girl he claimed to have met some four years earlier when he had been the one to drive the produce truck for Hans Baumholtz.

Had a stranger sitting in the Lee front room asked Lighthorse the whereabouts of the family, he would have replied that they were all somewhere close about. On second thought he would have explained that what he meant was that they had all been present such a short time before that it was perfectly natural to assume they were about to enter the room. But no stranger questioned Lighthorse, and he spent too much time waiting for the next hour to question himself.

The next hour was Nancy's hour with him or his hour with her, and on this evening *that hour* took them from her house up Walnut to Main and down Main across Cherry and out the path that led to the river bank, to the privacy of the beach where they stretched out in the warm sand to watch the sun sink and the moon rise. They lay a short distance apart, not speaking, not desiring to speak, watching the slow movement of the river and the few fleet bass that surfaced to snatch the white winged insects wandering low across the green-tinted water. When the shadows of night crept from out of the woods across the river and met the shadows from their side, shadows from the huge pile of sand on which they lay, Lighthorse rolled over to place his hand on Nancy's.

Still neither spoke, and only return pressure from her fingers expressed her acceptance of him. But when the three-quarter moon had driven the shadows as far back as it could drive them, Nancy said, "There's something I'd like to explain, Lighthorse—about us. You don't mind if I talk?" Her eyes were searching his face in the half light.

"Speak! Speak!" Lighthorse piped, imitating the sound of the half-dozen nighthawks that took their toll of high-flying insects above their heads.

"Well, it has already caused so much misunderstanding I wasn't sure."

"Misunderstanding is hereby outlawed forever," Lighthorse said. "Repeat after me: *entre nous es ist.*"

"*Entre nous,*" Nancy said, "and I . . ."

"Sorry!" Lighthorse interrupted. "The code is *entre nous es ist.*"

"Oh fiddle! We sound like my mother and father."

"*Entre nous es ist.* I do your French, you must do my German."

"*Entre nous es ist,* damn you! And I want you to hear the truth just in case someone tells you—makes up a big lie."

"I don't listen to big lies—ever. Now little ones. . ."

"Okay! But I want you *to know* I didn't tell Ted Biggers the story you told me. I didn't tell him anything except that you had told me a wonderful legend about an Indian maid and her lover."

"That was kid stuff," Lighthorse said, dismissing the subject.

"You didn't think so once."

"But you did."

"No, I didn't, Lighthorse. Never. I thought it was a *marvelous* story, the nicest I ever heard." She stopped. "Would you—would you want me to explain how I came to tell Ted Biggers about it—just by name. I'd never tell anyone your story." She waited and then went on. "Ted is a . . . a driving person, Lighthorse. He's very insistent when he wants anything, and he'll go to just about any length—"

"Go on—he wanted you!"

"I suppose so. I'd gone out sleighing with him, just a week after you and I took our walk. We went out to Shoenfelder's Hill with Steve Owens and Phil Arkwright and those P. K. Smith girls—Jenny and Lucy."

"The red-haired Smith sisters with the middy blouses.

Their old man's cracked, and if it involves them I'd rather you didn't tell me," Lighthorse said. "Those two have tough enough times."

"I know—and so do all preacher's kids—but I want you to hear it. Steve Owens drove us out in his dad's Chrysler; Ted and Phil had their sleds tied on behind the car, and Ted and Phil and Lucy and I rode them out. Steve drove slow and it was a nice ride banging back and forth—"

"Two of you on each sled?"

"Yes. Ted was sitting with me, and Phil held Lucy. The ride out was all right, but when we got to Schoenfelder's Hill, we found the snow too deep for sleighing—I guess I should have known that, at least Lucy and Jenny said they didn't want to ride sleds all night anyway."

"I *wish* you'd just skip it, Nance."

"No." Nancy went on: "We built a fire and—and the fellows had a jug of wine they kept going to the car to drink, and they had some blankets. Lucy and Phil and Jenny and Steve were soon all wrapped up—you know."

Lighthorse had piled up a little house of sand, but he swept it aside.

"That left Ted and me pretty much alone," Nancy said, "too much alone, I guess. Ted had ideas too, and I had to hold him off. I went back to the car, but he got in the back seat with me—I didn't get the door locked in time." Nancy's voice had gone slightly high.

"Ted Biggers did this to you?" Lighthorse asked, digging his hands deep into the sand at his side.

"Ted wasn't entirely to blame. He had had too much to drink, and he had the example of Phil and Steve—well, you know."

"Maybe I don't run with the right people—for examples."

"Lighthorse, don't say that. Don't be that way. I'm telling

123

you everything so you'll know"—Nancy's voice broke—
"everything. I did finally get him stopped. I had to bite his
hand, but I got him stopped, and then you'll never believe
what happened next."

"What?"

"He began to cry. Maybe it was only a crying jag or
maybe his hand hurt—it was bleeding—but he began to
cry and say he was sorry and so on and so on."

"Is that when you told him about—us?"

"I didn't tell him about us except in this way: I told him
he'd get a lot farther with a girl if he told her a beautiful
story instead of trying to rape her."

"Rape?"

"Rape! On the back seat of a car in freezing weather with
a drunk attacking you, you say what you mean. I may have
cussed a little too."

Lighthorse took her hand.

"I told him he'd get much farther by telling a girl a story
such as the one you told me. I just said it was a beautiful
legend of an Indian maid named Pink Tongue and her lover
and that you were going to test the legend someday. I told
him that, just that, a couple of times, and he listened finally,
and then he apologized. He apologized and then I helped
him tie up his hand. And I put some blankets around him
and shut the car doors and sat beside him, and we waited."

"I think you were kind," Lighthorse said. "Really kind—
to him and me." As Nancy talked he had been thinking he
would beat up Ted Biggers, but now he gave up the idea.

"I only did what I had to do."

"I guess I was the childish one. I mean my running out of
class and then calling you a damned fool and ignoring you.
Why in the world didn't you tell me this earlier?"

"I couldn't, you didn't give me a chance, and I didn't
have the nerve."

"I'm glad you have the nerve now." Lighthorse got to his feet.

"I've got you now." Nancy swung her hand and caught his.

"That's true." Lighthorse closed both hands on hers. "I wonder how long your infatuation will last?"

"You dog!" She hooked both hands and yanked, pulling him off balance. She leaped to her feet and started running.

When he caught up with her, they walked side by side along the path that led back to Main Street, but when they reached Cherry, he turned her right toward the cemetery. They stopped to explore the locust tree containing the embedded tomahawk. Lighthorse told her about it, as they walked. They circled the grass plot enclosing the mound that marked the burial spot of the ninety Christian Indians and went toward the willow trees that clung to the steep river bank.

They sat on a rock, the very rock from which Clem Philips said the Indian maid had made her death plunge, and then Lighthorse announced in self-mockery: "One thing has puzzled me a good bit about your evening with Ted Biggers, Nancy. Nothing about you and him, but what you told him about the way to win a girl. You said to tell her a legend, and by your own admission I told you a legend. I told you a legend once before, and I told you another here tonight."

"You did."

"Well—I consider your statement—"

"Lighthorse, you kill me!" Nancy laid her leg against his and let her body descend slowly. "Now look, Simon Legree," her lips when she spoke were brushing his, "when you want me you just tell me a legend, but don't turn into a merchant driving a bargain." She kissed him and stood up.

He caught her waist but her hands on his chest stopped

him. "Don't do it, Daddy, or I'll jump!" In pantomime she sent the legendary Indian maid toward the moonlit water below.

"I can dive too," he whispered as they wrestled one another.

"And I can bite," she said, her face close to his. "Remember that apple I stole from you and des-e-crated."

"I'm glad you didn't say, 'Remember Ted Biggers,' or I'd have known you meant it." Their lips met again.

"This can't go on," she said when she was free to breathe. "You haven't even kept your promise."

"What promise?"

"You told me you would test the legend of the Indian maid."

"Stuff!" he scoffed.

"You won't test it—ever?"

"You mean you dare me?"

"I don't mean anything, I just asked."

"It's a deal!" Off came his shirt, his tanned shoulders gleaming bronze in the moonlight. "Don't mind my trousers," he said as he loosened his belt and kicked off trousers, shorts, shoes and socks.

"Lighthorse!"

"You can always look the other way if it annoys you."

"You aren't serious? Please, Lighthorse, don't be ridiculous. You can't even judge the distance—and you don't know how deep the water is even if you make it. Darling, please!"

She was still talking as he stepped to the rock and sent his body hurtling into space. He knew he was being foolish—but he also knew it was right. It had to be. It was right and he was proving the legend—this as his lungs filled in flight and his hands and arms broke water for his head and he slipped down, down, down, and his arms and legs moved in frog-kick to send him in a blind search of the river's depths. On and on he swam in underwater search, until his lungs began to jerk, his eyes to bulge, his brain to thud in need of air, and he had to move upward and surface at last.

Three-quarters of the way across the river and slightly downstream from his starting point he surfaced, gulped air, treaded water, and called out: "Nancy, it's a hoax. There's no maiden—there's no—hey!"

He was off toward her, his back cleaving water, sailfish fashion, "Nance, Nance, you sweetheart!" he exclaimed a moment later as their bodies pushed aside the warm sheet of water.

"What? What did you yell?" She brushed back her streaming hair.

"Never mind, I was just saying the legend's a hoax."

"It wouldn't need be," she said, kissing him, her breasts against his chest, her arms embracing him, the two of them treading water with feet only.

"You were awful silly to risk that dive," she said, and having spoken her reprimand, she let herself slip underwater, all the way down against him, so that her hair wrapped his feet.

He waited and then touched his face upon her face. "You were even more silly to follow me in."

"I didn't dive. I splashed in from the bank." She locked her hands on his shoulders and drew him under against her.

He shot up beside her. "Well it's nice of you to be here."

"You too!" She was laughing. "Your love-li-ness increaseth!" she exclaimed as the water poured in her mouth.

He raised her against him hungrily.

She settled there for the moment. Then she pushed back her hair and patted it to rid it of water, and rolled over to take a few strokes upstream. "I could always swim off— join the other Indian maiden."

"But I love you, and so you won't."

She raised her hand to her ear. "What did you say?"

"I love you—always have, always will—as if you didn't know, couldn't guess." He caught her and treading water, raised her so that his lips brushed hers, and her neck and her breasts beneath the waterfall of her hair.

"You do, and I do," she whispered.

He lay back and pulled her upon him. "You will?"

She pushed him under and swam away from him, laughing.

His eyes followed her slender body, its curves lending grace to her motion, and when he swam by her side, she turned toward the far shore where a sandbar jutted into the moonlit river.

≥ 22 ≤

The family was at supper, and Mr. Lee turned his head sufficiently to see the car that had pulled up in front of the house. "Somebody—why, I believe it's Mr. Sutton in his ever-loving Buick," he said to Mrs. Lee, beginning to get up from the table.

"Did he get a new car?" Mrs. Lee asked. "It catches the sun so I can hardly see it."

"No. He certainly takes care of the old one, though. I find him washing or waxing and polishing it practically every morning when I go to work."

"At six a.m., oh dear! And he says Mrs. Sutton has her problems." Mrs. Lee turned to Lighthorse. "Do sit down and give him a chance to come to the door."

Lighthorse had heard the car stop too, and a quick glance over his shoulder had told him that the visitor was indeed Mr. Sutton, and now he was on his feet, his hand on the screen door. "Don't mind me, I'm almost done. He probably wants to see me—I mean he might want to see me." His voice wasn't at all his own as he crossed the porch to try to head Mr. Sutton off before he got around the car. There was no alternative; in his mind Mr. Sutton could be coming only about the swimming, and he had to head him off.

"Mr. Sutton, sir," he said, his hand reaching for Mr. Sutton's arm. "I—I guess you want to see me." He was blocking the little walk as he spoke, but Mr. Sutton stepped around him, moving to the porch.

"No Lighthorse, I wanted to speak to your parents—are they in?"

"They're at supper. Dad's been working late again. I mean he just sat down; if you—wanted to talk—" Lighthorse motioned vainly toward the car.

Mr. Sutton stopped. "This is a matter for your parents, Lighthorse. Your mother—is she available?"

"She's eating too. They just sat down. I mean I eat faster than anyone, Hessie or Hube or anyone. If it's—if you really have to talk to Mom and Dad I wish you'd give me a chance to say something first."

"You're very kind," Mr. Sutton said. "But I'd rather discuss this affair privately. I rather imagine you have a way of working your will with your folks, Lighthorse, and this is something I want them to accept or reject solely as a business arrangement."

"A business arrangement?"

"It'll have to be that," Mr. Sutton said. "I won't have it otherwise. Now I know charity grows in the grain here, but where Mrs. Sutton is concerned. . ."

"Mrs. Sutton—you mean you need to see Mom and Dad about Mrs. Sutton?" Lighthorse saw the sky suddenly assume its proper height, the evening sun assume a smiling face. He stepped aside and ushered Mr. Sutton across the porch and into the front room, calling toward the dining room, "Mom and Dad, Mr. Sutton wants to see you."

130

"Please take your time," Mr. Sutton called out. "I'm in no hurry and I wouldn't think of calling you from the table."

"But we're done," Mr. Lee said, entering the room. "I was just finishing my coffee as you drove up."

Mr. Sutton looked at Lighthorse and Lighthorse said: "Dad's a fast eater too. I got my speed at the table from him."

"What I came to talk about is this matter I mentioned when I brought the laundry last time, this matter involving Selma," Mr. Sutton said, after Mrs. Lee had come into the room and they were seated. "I hope we can keep it private," he added, glancing toward the dining room.

Lighthorse motioned outside: "Hessie and Hube and I can disappear. Get in an evening round of croquet."

"You almost read my mind," Mr. Sutton said as Lighthorse moved to go.

"I wouldn't say exactly," Lighthorse spoke from the doorway where he held the door and beckoned Hessie. Hubert had gone out the back door and stood waiting in the side yard.

When Mr. Sutton had gone that night, Mr. Lee asked them to step into the front room. His tone told them that a family conference was about to take place.

"It's just sensible for them to know about such a thing whatever you decide to do," he was saying to Mrs. Lee as they crossed the porch.

"Mr. Sutton wanted some discretion used—there's Hessie," Mrs. Lee said.

"When we can't trust them, Hessie or any one of them, then we'll just toss discretion to the hogs," Mr. Lee said. "Come here, kids. What your mother and Mr. Sutton and I have been talking about is a matter for all of us to decide." They sat down and while he reached out a hand and gently tugged at Hessie's hair, Mr. Lee explained Mr. Sutton's desire to hire Mrs. Lee as a part-time housekeeper and companion for Mrs. Sutton. Mrs. Sutton was not any better following her stay in the sanitarium, and her husband had reason to fear for her life.

"Why in the world does he pick on Mom?" Hessie asked. "I'd say he's got his nerve."

"Hessie!" Mrs. Lee said.

"Well, I don't care—"

"Let me finish," Mr. Lee went on. "Mrs. Sutton herself asked that Mary come to be with her. Mr. Sutton said he tried to talk her out of it but she insists."

"She insists?" Hessie said.

"It looks to me like Missus Sutton's had her way too often already," Hubert said.

"I don't think you understand," Mr. Lee said. "You can't do much with a person in Mrs. Sutton's condition. The time to handle her firmly has long since passed. Like most mentally ill people, she finds the siding leading nowhere much more appealing than the main line."

"That's not the way I'd say it," Hubert said. "She's just a drunken bum and she knows it and old Mutton Sutton knows it. Then because they've got a goddamn bank full of money they go parading around saying she's sick and be careful to let her do what she wants or she'll hurt herself. If it was my doing I'd give her a gun; if she used it, so much the better."

"Hubert, you're a hard man," Mr. Lee said. "You've got the makings of a Methodist circuit rider. Too bad that vocation closed when I was a young man."

"What really is wrong with Mrs. Sutton?" Lighthorse asked, fixing his eyes on his father, but thinking "Nancy, Nancy."

"You're more intimately tied up with that damned family than any of us," Hubert snapped. "Why don't you tell us?"

"I wish I could," Lighthorse said. "Boy, I wish I could—for her sake and Nancy's. I know she thinks Nancy and Mr. Sutton combine against her, make it hard for her. But she thinks that about almost everyone. I know she needs help, I know that."

"She certainly does," Mrs. Lee put in.

"But I'm not sure you should have to help her." Lighthorse looked at his mother and then turned to Hubert. "Most things in life aren't your little cushy right and wrong either, Hube."

"You're telling me!" Hubert exclaimed. "Brother, you're telling me! Mrs. Sutton is really a dirty gray—a dirty gray alley cat, if you really want to know." His voice became brittle and bitter. "Look Dad, why don't you quit beating around the goddamn bush and tell us exactly why Sutton came over *here*, to talk to you and Mom about that old bag."

For the first time in his life Lighthorse saw both his father and mother in mental rout. It was as if they had been dealt a blow simultaneously, a blow which dulled their clear eyes that ordinarily spoke before their voices and gave the particular independent quality to the words they uttered. In their eyes, pride and loss of pride—and Lighthorse realized that his mother had been holding back in all the conversation. Now she spoke: "Hubert, I wish you wouldn't be vicious. There's no need for that, no need at all. Nat," she said, as if resigned to the inevitable, "you might just as well speak frankly now that we've gone this far."

"It's all around town!" Hubert snorted. "Has been for months."

"What's around town?" Hessie asked.

Lighthorse said nothing but he had the same question.

"All right," Mr. Lee said. "It's true that Ed and Mrs. Sutton were carrying on an affair. How he ever got mixed up with her is beyond me, but he did. And Mr. Sutton acted very diplomatically in sending Mrs. Sutton away. But she wouldn't stay away; she attempted suicide and they had to bring her home again. And all we could do is what we did: we had Elmo take Ed out of town when she came back."

"So that's why Elmo gave up his job," Lighthorse said.

"Of course not! He left town for his health," Hubert exclaimed. "And just when he had a chance to work in the office at the clay plant. He could have begun to use his mind instead of his back."

"Elmo did it of his own free will," Mrs. Lee said defensively. "He suggested it, and did it. He thought it was the only thing to do. He even said he owed Mr. Sutton a debt of gratitude for bringing him in one time—you remember, that time he got drunk and Mr. Sutton helped him home—you all remember that."

"Sure we remember, and so you unload the family troubles onto good old Elmo." Hubert turned to his father: "I told you it was wrong when you were doing it."

"I did the only thing I could do," Mr. Lee exclaimed angrily. "Everett and Elmo both said so."

"I didn't," Hubert muttered.

"When did all this happen—you didn't even tell me," Hessie said, beginning to cry. "You just do everything without me and then somebody will come up to me in the street and say something mean. No wonder the kids all look at me the way they do."

"I didn't know anything about it either," Lighthorse said to Hessie. If Hessie felt this way, how were people treating Nancy? In his happiness he had been bat-blind. He looked at his father and shook his head.

"My god," Mr. Lee said, "please don't act like this. Don't you all see we're trying to do the best we can under the circumstances? It's not my fault Ed got mixed up with that bitch."

"Nat!" Mrs. Lee said.

"Well, that's the only term for her," Mr. Lee said. "And to think I told that boy—I made him walk her home. That's being the good Samaritan with a capital 'S.'"

"What I'd like to know is why the devil we even talk about Mom going over there to look after her," Hubert said. He grabbed a loose cushion that Mr. Lee had knocked off the sofa and beat it into the floor. "I don't see how you could think of going," he said to his mother.

"Think of going—of course I'll go if I need to go," Mrs. Lee said.

"You'd go simply to make sure she didn't get near Ed again?" Lighthorse asked, wondering if her sacrifice had no limit. "Mom," he went on, "I wish you'd not do that. I can't quite understand how Mr. Sutton could come here—could have the guts to ask you."

"That's exactly what I said," Hubert exclaimed.

"You forget one thing." Mr. Lee's tone acknowledged he was fighting a lost cause. "That woman's desperate. She'll do something tragic and then we'll think this—all this—is just a comedy. Mr. Sutton's no fool and he says she's desperate."

"Can't somebody lock her up?" Hessie said.

"Lock her up!" Hubert cried. "Why should they? She'd be better off if they handed her a gun and told her to do something desperate, something as desperate as blowing out her own brains—or his."

"I don't know," Lighthorse said, his head a whirl of pictures of Nancy and her parents, of Elmo and Ed, "I don't know what would be right, but I don't think you should go, Mom."

"Well, that settles it," Mr. Lee said, but with none of his old-time assurance. "Everett said that Elmo and Ed were getting along fine last week—"

"You mean Ev doesn't go to Pittsburgh to see his girl at all?" Lighthorse asked. "You mean he goes to Pittsburgh to check up on Ed—to see how Elmo is managing? Now is that what he's really doing?"

"More or less," Mrs. Lee said.

"So what if it is!" Mr. Lee said. His jaw muscles flexed as he fixed Lighthorse with a malevolent stare.

"Oh please. Nat, Lighthorse—please, let's all shut up."

Mr. Lee got up and walked toward the living room. He avoided even his wife's eyes as he did so, and Lighthorse noticed he was really a little man, a little, bald man somewhat stooped from too much hard physical labor. Lighthorse was almost certain he had walked much more erect an hour before, but because of the revelations of the past hour, he couldn't be sure.

Later that night Lighthorse awakened from nightmare-filled sleep to hear his mother weeping. The sound as it rolled out in endless waves of despair was too much to bear. He got up from his bed, crossed the room and tiptoed toward the door of his parents' bedroom. He was about to knock, anything to stop that sound, when he heard his father's voice low-pitched and comforting.

He returned to his bed, pulled the pillow across his face, and felt tears form and fall with muted sounds upon the mattress. The pillow above his head was not sufficient to shut out the sound of his mother's weeping. He finally lunged from his bed, dressed, and crept down the darkened stairs to escape into the night.

❧ 23 ❦

In mid-afternoon Lighthorse was at work in Hans Baumholtz's melon patch, lifting the thick-veined fruit with practiced hands to see if the stems pulled free at finger pressure, signifying perfect ripeness for shipping, when he saw Hank running across the field. He knew Hank should have been at home in bed resting for his night drive to Pittsburgh, yet he was not surprised; he sensed why Hank was coming for him. He didn't have the precise details, but he knew—and he straightened with a firm-ripe melon in each hand and bowled them gently toward the waiting shipping crate before he went to meet his brother.

"Mom sent me after you," Hank said. "She wants you to come right home. Elmo's hurt—Ed sent a telegram."

Lighthorse said: "I'll get my shirt and tell Mr. Baumholtz." He leaped across the few rows of sprawling melon vines and spoke to Hans Baumholtz. He snatched up his cast-off shirt from the many draped over the melon crates and followed Hank, toward the farm pickup truck Hank drove when he went home to take his nap before making a night trip.

"What happened?" Lighthorse asked, climbing in beside Hank. "You said Elmo's hurt?"

"I don't know the details—I didn't read the telegram." Hank was shifting gears and the wheels were spinning in loose sand as the truck started.

"Is he—he isn't bad hurt?"

"I don't know, I guess so. Ed sent the telegram saying Elmo is in a Pittsburgh hospital. Dad and Mom are going and they're taking you along."

"Taking me?"

"Mom said she wanted you along."

"Maybe Elmo asked—didn't you read the telegram?"

"I said I didn't read it. Goddammit, let up, won't you. Mom just yanked me out of bed and told me to get you." Hank spoke without removing his eyes from the road. They were doing sixty-ish—all the truck would do—and Hank said no more until they slowed and turned off Main Street. "I think it's a good idea for you to go. Mom and Dad'll need you."

"Sure," Lighthorse said. "Sure. Thanks, Hank."

Inside the front door Lighthorse found his father and mother already dressed, a suitcase packed, his grey Sunday suit laid out with his black oxfords and socks, along with a freshly ironed white shirt and a dark green tie belonging to Hubert.

"Hurry now," Mr. Lee said. "We'll catch the three-thirty-five out of Dennison if you hurry."

"Should I take a bath?" Lighthorse asked, going toward the kitchen.

"I don't know—you haven't much time."

"I'll smell less like a billy goat if I do," Lighthorse said as he moved to the washstand and began splashing soapy water under his arms and across his chest.

"You'll not be the first person who smelled of honest sweat," Mrs. Lee said, handing him a clean pair of shorts and an undershirt, and pulling the door shut after her.

Within five minutes they were on their way, the four of them crammed into the cab of the Ford pickup, the bulging suitcase sliding around in the rear. Lighthorse held his mother on his lap; his father sat pale and small in the middle, and Hank had the speedometer bouncing between sixty-two and sixty-five. While they waited at a stoplight in Uhrichsville half a mile from the Dennison station, Mr. Lee, who had his watch in hand, said, "We won't make it."

When they came to the tracks a quarter of a mile before the station, the watchman was signaling for traffic to stop, but Hank ignored him and somehow got across so that they raced the train itself into the station.

"Well, Hank boy, we made it," Mr. Lee said. "I didn't think we would make it, but we did." He repeated the sentence as Hank handed Lighthorse the suitcase. "You take care of Hubert and Hessie, Hank," Mrs. Lee said as they crossed the tracks and climbed into the day coach.

"Okay," Hank called. "Don't worry about anything," he added as the train started.

The ride into Pittsburgh gave Lighthorse a chance to bring order to his mind, a chance to note that his mother had once again summoned an amazing strength. Only the fullness of her dark eyes indicated that this was other than a mission of pleasure. And her voice when she said, "Nat, I've got our annual passes here in my purse, but you'll have to pay Lighthorse's fare," was controlled and calm.

His father again struck Lighthorse as a little man he hardly knew. His efforts to do something with his gnarled hands, the way he locked them together, and set one thumbnail scraping the other told how completely unnerved he was. As he reached for his wallet and had difficulty extracting it from his pocket, Lighthorse saw that his tenseness had destroyed his coordination.

"I've got plenty of money, Dad," Lighthorse said. "You must never forget I'm a highly paid melon picker."

"Now where's that blamed telegram?" Mr. Lee said as he gave up on his wallet and began feeling through the pockets of his blue serge suit.

"It's in your shirt pocket, Nat," Mrs. Lee said. "You told me to put it there while you dressed, remember?"

"Well—" Mr. Lee found it and opened it. "Now it says Mount Gilead Hospital. I wonder how we'll get there?"

"We could ask someone in the station," Mrs. Lee said.

"Maybe a cab driver—we can afford a cab," Lighthorse said, feeling his wallet, which held the summer's earnings he had saved to buy his school clothes.

"Maybe they won't let us in—" Mr. Lee said and added awkwardly, "I guess we can always tell them who we are and why we came."

"Sure," Lighthorse said. "We'll get in all right. Don't worry."

"Nat," Mrs. Lee said as she moved over to sit beside Lighthorse, facing her husband, "why don't you just stretch out there on the seat and try to get a little sleep? We've got a three-hour ride and you're completely worn out."

"Maybe I could," Mr. Lee said. He took off his suitcoat and folded it over the arm of the seat. "Of course the conductor will be along for the tickets—for our passes and a ticket for Elmo—Everett—Ed—Lighthorse!" He grimaced. "Of course, for Lighthorse."

"I've got our passes ready," Mrs. Lee said, her hand on

140

her purse. "You just stretch out. Here—" She stood up and took off her coat and put it on top of his coat, making a pillow for his head.

"I'll pay my own fare," Lighthorse repeated to his mother. "I can pay for the cab and things too."

"We might even need a hotel room, I suppose," Mrs. Lee said, lowering her voice.

"I can pay for that too," Lighthorse said. "I've got thirty-four dollars."

"If he just isn't too seriously hurt—" Mrs. Lee spoke almost to herself.

"Elmo's plenty strong; I don't think he could be hurt seriously," Lighthorse said. "I remember—" he glanced at his mother and let his voice die away.

"It's too bad Nat has to face this right now," she said. "He's asleep, poor dear. He hasn't been himself for some time."

"He looked worn out that night," Lighthorse said. "I wish to God Hube and I hadn't said so much."

"You both meant all right. You were just taking out on Dad what you couldn't take out on others."

There was a silence and Lighthorse said, "Mom, you could get some sleep too if you like." He got up and traded places with her. "Here, I'll take the passes. I guess the conductor's asleep too."

"Yes." Mrs. Lee nodded, smiled, and settled her head on her arm against the window.

She too was sound asleep before Lighthorse heard the conductor calling "Tickets, tickets," as he made his way through the neighboring car. Three quick steps and Lighthorse was able to hush the conductor. He saw his mother and father stir in their sleep but not awaken as he showed their passes and negotiated for his own ticket.

"That'll be two dollars and eighty cents." Quietly the conductor wrote out the ticket and quietly he moved down the aisle.

Lighthorse settled back to watch while his parents slept. He didn't bother to awaken them until the train entered Union Station, and then he carried the suitcase and got them into a cab and on the way to the hospital before either one was fully awake.

At the Mount Gilead Hospital, a white stone building blackened by coal smoke and lying just off the noisiest, busiest street Lighthorse had ever seen, he left them in the lounge while he spoke, telegram in hand, to the receptionist.

Then he had to go back and explain to them, as the receptionist told him to do—that the head nurse wanted to talk to them. The head nurse, a heavy-set woman of about fifty with faded red hair and a round motherly face, wore a blue cardigan sweater over her nurse's uniform, and smiled as she shook hands with his mother and father and pointed to the chairs.

"Mr. and Mrs. Lee," she said in a low voice, "I know of no easy way to say what I have to say. Your son—the one who was shot—died at midnight; the other one—the one who was with him until he died—has arranged to take the body to the Dirskin Funeral Home."

Lighthorse noticed his mother's mouth open just enough for an indrawn breath; he saw his father's gnarled thumbs, nail scraping against nail, and then he heard his mother murmur, "You mean Elmo is dead—shot to death?"

"He died of his wounds," the red-haired nurse said. "He was shot in the head, he couldn't have lived; it was just a matter of time."

"But you say Elmo was *shot?*" Mr. Lee said. "Where was he that he was shot?"

"He was shot by a woman who came to their boarding-house. Your other son was with him at the time."

"A woman—a woman shot Elmo?" Mrs. Lee said. "But what woman would do that?"

"She turned the gun on herself and took her own life," the nurse explained. "Your other son has gone to the police station to make a statement, I believe. I know he identified the woman." She glanced at the record on her desk. "Her name was Sutton, Selma Sutton."

"Mrs. Sutton!" Lighthorse exclaimed. "Oh, my God!" He turned to his parents but he was thinking of Nancy. His mother's face was hidden in her hands, and his father blew his nose vigorously and wiped at his eyes. The red-haired nurse was looking away, looking out the window, and she did not turn toward them until Mr. Lee stood up and said, "We're very grateful to you. Mary," he said, his hand on his wife's shoulder, "I think we should go now. We'll need to find Elmo—Everett—Edward!"

"Yes," Mrs. Lee said, "I suppose so. Yes, we'll have to find Edward."

"We'll go to the funeral home," Lighthorse mumbled.

The nurse, apparently about to say the same thing, nodded. "It's the Dirskin Funeral Home on Claremont Road. Your other son—Edward—may be there."

They were turning from the corridor into the reception room when a stocky figure in a light gray topcoat detached itself from the group entering the building. He removed his hat so that his bald head shone as he walked toward the receptionist.

Lighthorse whispered, "There's Mr. Sutton! He's probably hunting us—or his wife."

"Why it *is* Mr. Sutton," Mrs. Lee exclaimed. "Come, Nat, we'll have to speak to him—be especially kind to him."

"Things are all out of whack when a father has to bury his son," Mr. Lee murmured. "You expect a son to bury his father, not the other way around. Of course if there's a war, then a father has to expect to bury his son." He turned to Lighthorse. "But this isn't a war."

"Nat," Mrs. Lee said. "Come, we must speak to Mr. Sutton."

Mr. Lee went forward hesitantly, propelled and supported by Lighthorse's hand on his arm, and when Mr. Sutton saw them advancing, still some ten feet away, his glance of recognition gave way to one not unlike the one on Mr. Lee's face. Lighthorse stood aside as the two met and shook hands awkwardly. Mr. Sutton asked a question to which there was a one-word response by Mr. Lee, not an accusation, but an admission of defeat—and then like a blurred picture suddenly set in focus, the notion in Lighthorse's mind came clear: this was the meeting of the incompetents. Had he been an artist, he could have re-created the scene before him with its proper overtones—those overtones locked forever in the ivory and blue drapes of the window, blue tinted wall meeting window and moving to a slightly darker angle and then coming away lighted from the window, the meaning of two well-intentioned men beside the woman whose son they had accidentally slain.

Seized by despair because he could not erase what time had written, Lighthorse stepped forward and took the hand relinquished by his father, and then with a voice that reverberated from the ceiling and the walls, a voice that he knew to be his only because his mouth was open and the pressure of speech was upon his ears, Lighthorse said: "Elmo was the one you—your wife killed, you understand —Elmo!"

"Lighthorse!" Mrs. Lee said sharply. "Mr. Sutton lost someone near to him too."

Lighthorse dropped Mr. Sutton's hand and moved on to leave his accusation like a rootless tree. In the corner, he took his mother's arm, and heard her voice again, even though his eyes had carried him out of the room to the street where the spinning disc of a car wheel matched the haze in his mind. "I—I can't believe it. Elmo dead."

His mind constant to one image—the shoulders and head of Elmo—Lighthorse watched a gang of workmen stepping off a bus. He followed one set of legs and arms after another into nothingness, and each bore the shoulders and head of Elmo, the shoulders that rose in sinewy strength such as he had never seen in another, and the head his model for what a mind might be.

His mother was speaking reassurances as much by tone as phrase, and he was aware of her meaning without hearing her words: "He never thought of himself; he was the one at one with all of us."

"There is a tear no one can mend in this life."

"He had dreams, unselfish dreams for you."

"He and you were one piece and that piece lies broken."

"Nothing live can last."

She said, "Elmo would have wanted you here, even though it is hardest this way."

"Did you know he was dying?" Lighthorse asked.

"I—I can't say. It would be false to say I didn't sense it, although I denied it from the moment the telegram came."

"I'm glad of one thing." Lighthorse formed each word with care to be certain that she got precisely what he meant: "I'm glad you let me come . . . be here . . . with you and Dad."

"I think Mr. Sutton and Nat are waiting," she said.

145

They crossed the room and listened to Mr. Lee explain that Mr. Sutton had offered to take them to the Dirskin Funeral Home and to the boardinghouse. Mr. Sutton stood by like a chauffeur, without speaking.

PART FOUR

1937

≫ 24 ≪

Selma Sutton was buried from the Moravian Church and Elmo Lee from the Methodist on successive days, their graves not a hundred feet apart, to the south and west of the limestone monument that marked the final resting place of the Indian martyrs. Lighthorse returned to work on the Baumholtz produce farm, returned to pick the golden melons that showed too green one day, were firm-ripe for three or four, and then cracked to admit the melon bugs and flies. He walked upon the sandy loam that felt springy with life and promise of life, but which he knew had recently partaken of death. And seeing his mother and father withdrawn and broken; seeing Ed staggering between house and town; seeing Everett, Hank, and Hubert grow loud-mouthed in response to gossip about Mrs. Sutton and Ed; seeing Hessie's eyes etched dark and large from the same cause—seeing all this and sensing that Nancy and Mr. Sutton suffered from the same blight, Lighthorse could only crouch within himself and wait.

He had spoken to Mr. Sutton and Nancy at the funerals, but fearful he could at best heap on pain, he had decided to have as little to do with them as possible. Feeling himself ancient at the age of seventeen, he walked to school to begin the year, signed up for his courses, and entered the daily routine of class and study hall, and again roamed the warm, well-lighted halls and sat in the cozy classrooms, dejected and defeated, yet with a mind charged by that promise Mr. Spiker and Miss Tillotson had seen in him.

Fall fled in heavy rain and wild winds, and as the Lee kitchen with its huge cast-iron cookstove failed to become the haven it had been, Lighthorse spent more and more time at school. Most of that time he spent reading in Mr. Spiker's private library. Mr. Spiker had called Lighthorse to his office after the two of them had gone at one another with no holds barred in the Problems of Democracy class.

"Lighthorse, you gave me a rough time this morning," Mr. Spiker began, indicating a chair beside his and swinging his own swivel chair so that the desk no longer separated them.

"Not really," Lighthorse murmured, and then catching the light in Mr. Spiker's eyes, he added: "I'm sorry."

"I'm not. I stuck out my chin and you swung. Aided and abetted by that witty Nancy Sutton you made me look a little ridiculous too." Mr. Spiker was rubbing the bridge of his nose with a bent finger.

"I'm sure the class didn't think that."

"Who gives a damn what the class thinks—if it does think," Mr. Spiker said. "Lighthorse, you're the second student I've met in fifteen years at this school who has guts enough to think and speak—to expose our clichés to the test of your own thinking."

"I was just trying—oh, you know." Lighthorse waved his

hand in disclaimer. "Once I thought that if life dealt you short in one way, it dealt you long in something else— maybe energy, or persistence, or health—or even family. I don't believe that anymore."

"In questioning begins wisdom—if I remember my philosophy," Mr. Spiker said. "Before I got sidetracked by Nancy Sutton's sashay into women's rights, I was going to qualify my statement that men and women are born free and equal in these United States by saying we're born free and equal in the eyes of the law. What would you say to that?"

"I'd say it isn't true."

"Lighthorse"—whimsy lightened Mr. Spiker's voice— "you wouldn't call me a liar?"

Lighthorse met Mr. Spiker's eyes. "We could wish men and women were born equal before the law. Some of that— equality for whites, I mean—may have been the hope of those who wrote the Bill of Rights. But they had their limitations."

"Their sexual and white-skin bondage, I think Nancy put it."

"Yes. Their sexual and racial bias—I guess she named it 'sexual bent and white-skin bondage.' But just think about equality before the law." Lighthorse paused. "Do you know where my brother Ed is right now? He's in the county jail for driving while intoxicated. Has been for two days."

"I'm sorry to hear that."

"He's the one in jail, the one 'the law'—read 'Judge Barnes'—says needs a little time to think things over. But recall Mrs. Sutton and the time she crashed the red light and knocked old Henry Peterson down. She was so drunk she couldn't stand and what became of her? She was taken home by Judge Barnes himself. Even before Doc Spears examined her, Judge Barnes said she was having her month-lies and had suffered a fainting spell. She was never charged with any crime."

"I think Mrs. Sutton's was an unusual case—and evidently that's one instance of neither sexual bent nor white skin bias . . ."

"Bank book bias," Lighthorse said. "And there's another case closer to home. You remember last spring, when Peter Arkwright discovered somebody stealing gasoline from the pump he uses for his trucks. He lay in wait a few nights and charged out after them, and got shot in the leg. You remember who the 'someones' were?"

"That was serious business all the way around." Mr. Spiker cleared his throat.

"Well, no crime was committed, or at least the investigation was stopped. Of course, anyone who wasn't blind saw Horace Biggers and Harold Owens sneaking down the alleys almost every night to make arrangements with Pete Arkwright about the doctor bill and all. I'll bet Doc Spears could tell some details on that one that would make equality before the law look pretty wispy."

"You would agree that this last—this gunshot case—was settled for the best interests of all concerned. Those two boys wouldn't be a bit better off if they'd have spent time in the reformatory."

"I'd hope not," Lighthorse said. "But what equal law says my brother Ed will be better because of his stay in the county jail but they—you see my point?"

"Certainly, certainly." Mr. Spiker sat back musing, massaging the bridge of his nose, his eyes half closed. "I guess you have a right to be bitter. I'm glad things turned out as they did—in class, I mean. You and Nancy Sutton argued a pretty convincing, even enlightening, case, I'd say."

"I always thought the family—Mom and Dad and all of us living together—sort of made up for this other," Lighthorse said quietly. "Now after Elmo paid his life for the way the law favored Mrs. Sutton, I'm not sure. In fact, Ed and all of us are still paying part of the same bill."

"Lighthorse," Mr. Spiker said, "I think you're going to reverse these judgments someday. Not that you'll ever fall for this equality pap. But someday you're going to thank your lucky stars you were born into the situation you were. Someday I think you'll find yourself achieving your dreams, Lighthorse, and then you'll see some balance of reality and justice in your life."

Lighthorse started to protest but Mr. Spiker raised his hand, turned to one of a dozen books on his desk, and lifted out what appeared to be a random choice. The book, however, opened to the page he desired. He read:

> . . . if one advances confidently in the direction of his dreams, and endeavors to live the life which he has imagined, he will meet with a success unexpected in common hours. He will put some things behind, will pass an invisible boundary; new, universal, and more liberal laws will begin to establish themselves around and within him; or the old laws be expanded, and interpreted in his favor in a more liberal sense, and he will live with the license of a higher order of beings.

Mr. Spiker finished, but his slightly nasal voice reverberated, filling the office.

Lighthorse said: "I'd like to go along with that, but I just can't."

Mr. Spiker looked away as he repeated: "He will put some things behind—will pass an invisible boundary. . . ."

Lighthorse swallowed but said nothing.

"Well," Mr. Spiker cleared his throat, "forgetting our little contretemps, there's one law of equality I'd like to break right now." He reached into his pocket and drew out a ring of keys. He rolled the dozen of them around, searching for one particular key, and then worked it off the ring. "Now here's a key"—he repeated slowly "here's a key to that little room where my books are kept. There's a desk and a lamp in there—and this is only the second time I've ever made this offer." He glanced at Lighthorse and then at the key—and used his fingernail to pry a trifle of pocket lint off it. "I'd like you to take this key and use that office, Lighthorse. It's not exactly equality with the taxpayer's money," he was smiling, "but it would certainly make me feel good to know you were working at your own speed, with books I've read and liked."

He held out the key and Lighthorse took it, enclosed it in his fist. "Thanks, Mr. Spiker. Thanks a whole lot."

"By the way," Mr. Spiker added, "you'd never guess who it was that I offered that key to once before."

"Who?"

"Your brother Elmo in his senior year." Mr. Spiker sat back and laughed. "He gave me a typical Elmo Lee response too. He told me to stick the key."

"Elmo was proud," Lighthorse said, "more than proud." He rubbed the key between thumb and finger. "I'll take the key for him and me. I'll eat the crow."

"I'm the one who's eating crow—enjoying it," Mr. Spiker said. "I just wanted you to know that I knew Elmo for the guy he was."

❧ 25 ❦

Once he had an office, a steam-heated office with a small desk and bright lamp, and a straight-backed chair, an office lined with the best collection of books he had ever seen, and most of those sprinkled with comments and cross references in Mr. Spiker's fine hand—once he was in the heaven that office represented, Lighthorse's bitterness became impatience. He was impatient at home, with the time his small tasks about the house required, for he was responsible for tending his mother's flock of twenty-five hens and feeding the three foxhounds—two males and one female—Ed had acquired. But he was glad to do the chores too, especially since his mother had given up doing laundry and he no longer had to take time to help her with that, and he saw that Ed was becoming sufficiently interested in hunting and fishing to spend almost as much time in the fields as he did in the saloons in Uhrichsville and Dennison. And he knew the reason for his impatience at time spent away from the office: he was reading for two persons. He had to read for Elmo because this was Elmo's opportunity he was using, and he read for himself to keep pace with Elmo.

Impatient though he might be to get to The Stall, as the office got christened, he was never impatient while there. Rather, he was painstakingly thorough as he tied up men with ideas until he seized and held a great viable chain crossing time and space. Like an explorer—Keats' Balboa before the Pacific fixed in his mind—he saw more than met his eye and thrilled at all he saw.

After reading Saint Augustine and Cardinal Newman and in the midst of Gerard Manley Hopkins, absorbing ideas and words with something approaching physical appetite, he handed Mr. Spiker what he called his melon metaphor:

How like the word-world this melon is,
Where mere promises were, it is:
Sweet life, round-rolled, all His.
Thanking thus I taste the live-love He sent
Where cold hate was. Here all
Is green-got, gold-coiled, life-geared,
Led on to woo us, win us—
All of us—as His.

As he read and thought, and read to think again, he felt rise within him a wave of happiness that was physical in force, spiritual in intensity, and he felt anew his closeness to his brother Elmo.

Then on a mid-winter afternoon he fell asleep, head on arms, arms on books piled three deep on the desk, and as he slept he dreamed a bizarre yet satisfying dream in which he opened the door to admit Elmo to the comfort of The

154

Stall, to the intimacy of a small book that seemed to be being written even as he was reading it. He wanted to tell Elmo about the book but when he flipped back to the title page it was oddly blank. "Well?" he exclaimed.

And yet Elmo seemed to know the book, for he said: "I see you like The Book of Others—The Book of Parts. Sometimes the title varies, but it plays out the same: living and loving, taking others' faults, guilt, even death, taking it as our own. It's not easy—such living, such loving—but it must be done. There's no other way." Elmo's ruddy face grew luminously pale, the way Lighthorse had beheld it on the bier. He smiled and laid a hand on Lighthorse's shoulder. The hand was rock firm as it had been in death, but warm, not cold.

Repeated knocking at the door returned Lighthorse to The Stall.

"Mr. Sutton wanted to speak with you, Lighthorse," Mr. Spiker said. "I told him you were probably working on *our* books." To Mr. Sutton he added, "I think Lighthorse would sleep in The Stall, if we'd let him."

"I've been caught doing just that," Lighthorse said. He brushed back his hair and stood for Mr. Sutton to enter the room.

Mr. Spiker went on: "My apologies for the close quarters. I'll be in my office if you want to see me, Mr. Sutton."

"Thank you," Mr. Sutton said. "Well-well," he began as Lighthorse edged clear of the door and closed it. "Now I know what it's like to be on a submarine."

"I've adjusted to it, and now I like it very much," Lighthorse said. Picking up the submarine image, he indicated the hundred or so books to the right of the window. "I'm bringing the room into trim, more or less."

Mr. Sutton was scanning the titles, reading names. He

paused, then asked: "Does the school—you're cataloguing the books, aren't you?"

"In a way I am." Lighthorse had to smile. "These"—he motioned to the left of the window—"these are still to be read."

"Read—you mean you have to read each book to catalogue it? That's pretty expensive for the school, isn't it?" Mr. Sutton turned toward Lighthorse.

"Not really," Lighthorse said. "I'm just reading them—just reading them to turn the pages, I guess." Sensing that his voice was too sharp, his remark smart-alecky, he added, "They're Mr. Spiker's own books."

"Well," Mr. Sutton exclaimed, "as Teddy Roosevelt would have said, 'Bully for him and bully for you!'" He glanced out the window. "If someone had told me this was going on in our own high school, I wouldn't have believed it." He pushed aside a stack of books and sat on the edge of the desk. "Now all this ties in with what I was intending to ask you—what I wanted to talk with you about, Lighthorse."

Lighthorse straightened and leaned toward the window; he looked out upon the built-up roof of the gymnasium and across the expanse of tar and loose pea gravel to the yellow brick chimney of the incinerator at the rear of the building.

"I wanted to ask you about a personal matter," Mr. Sutton went on. "As Selma used to say, I've got the grace and touch of a grizzly bear, but here goes. What I wanted to know—and your reading almost gives me my answer—I wanted to know whether you still plan to go to college, and if so, what sort of school you want to attend?"

Lighthorse continued to stare at the chimney. His eyes limned the image of Elmo's sweating face, Elmo's damp soot-covered chest and arms. He did not speak.

"More specifically," Mr. Sutton went on, glancing down at his left foot discreetly clothed in a brown silk sock and a brown French-toed oxford, a foot which he had drawn up slightly for comfort, "more specifically, I wondered if you would consider my alma mater, Ohio University, down at Athens?" He began to swing his left foot back and forth, and the ticks-ticks of the shoe-lace striking the leather was the only sound in the room. He waited then added: "Ohio U's not like Ohio State, you know. None of that oversize, none of that overkill in athletics." He laughed. "Not that some of the alumni and a handful of the faculty don't want it—it's just that they can't achieve it, or at least haven't yet. Ohio U's the oldest college in the Northwest Territory. It was provided for even before Ohio became a state. Early on it supplied the state with a good many leaders—governors, legislators, educators—all that kind of thing. It isn't exactly a private college, but it's a good little school, and I sort of thought maybe you'd be interested—" He paused and waited, and finally said, "You don't have a bias against Ohio U., do you, Lighthorse?"

"Not at all," Lighthorse said, and then his mouth clamped shut as though the words had escaped of their own accord.

"Well, what I was coming to is this," Mr. Sutton said. "Nancy used to tell me a good bit about the plans your brother Elmo—the plans you had concerning college, and it seemed reasonable for me to speak to you about Ohio U. It has some pretty good facilities and a very good faculty. Of course Athens is a one-horse town, the kind of place you'd expect as county seat in a coal-mining county in Appalachia, but the people are friendly and—"

Mr. Sutton stopped, cleared his throat, and then added, "God, would you listen to me—that's not even what I meant to say. I guess I just can't say what I mean, but what I was coming to is this, Lighthorse. Ohio U.—which I attended for better or for worse—is the college Nancy thinks she would like to attend, and to be perfectly frank, I'd like nothing better than to be paying two tuitions at one time— that is, if you think it would be agreeable, Lighthorse."

Lighthorse let out his breath, then drew another and said, "It seems a little unusual but if you wanted to do it . . ."

"Good! You mean you'll go—you and Nancy together?"

"I don't mean anything of the kind," Lighthorse said, his voice rising. "As far as I'm concerned you can pay two hundred tuitions—after all, it is your college and the college Nancy thinks she will attend. Why don't you pay a couple hundred tuitions, Mr. Sutton? I think they'd like that."

"You're"—Mr. Sutton's hand at his mouth muffled his words—"you're being mean, son. Pretty damned mean."

Lighthorse stared into Mr. Sutton's eyes and saw that they were as bloodshot as he knew his own to be. It seemed to him that both Mr. Sutton and he needed sleep badly, and that every single thing either thought or said should be ignored, but he went on: "I'm sorry for that, Mr. Sutton. But I don't want you to misunderstand. I don't need or want any help from you anytime—now or ever."

Mr. Sutton got to his feet, landed heavily so that the floor echoed, and in that sound the building seemed to shake. "Well, that's about as final as final can be."

Lighthorse sensed that the building must be shaking and locked his eyes on the gymnasium roof and the smoke-blackened tower of the incinerator.

"I'm sorry I wasted your time," Mr. Sutton announced from the doorway.

"Forget it," Lighthorse said. He spoke without shifting his eyes from the scene across the tar roof, a dismal scene on a bright day, purgatory on this dull one. "A good view for a study window," Mr. Spiker had once remarked, "because it forces you to turn your eyes inward." Lighthorse had already turned his eyes inward and now he bounded to the door, but Mr. Sutton was at the top of the stairs headed down, his jaw set.

⤳ 26 ⤴

A week after Mr. Sutton's visit to The Stall, Lighthorse found first use for the red leatherette appointment calendar that rested on his desk. During his second day in The Stall he had come upon the calendar under a stack of books, and had gone with it in hand to Mr. Spiker's office, intending to leave it there. But Mr. Spiker wouldn't hear of it. Drumming a yellow pencil on the scribbled-over calendar on his own desk, he said: "The calendar in your hand goes with the territory—your new territory. When traveling in books it's easy to lose track of what is real, and a desk calendar will remind you of real time, real life."

Beneath the date—Tuesday, February 15, 1938—Lighthorse wrote: "Owe Mr. Sutton A. See to it. Explain M,H, OSU." He paused, touched his pen to his chin, glanced out the window at the mauve afternoon sky, and wrote: "What about OU?"

A desk calender lets *me* hold the real world at bay, he thought, as he turned to take up the book he had been reading when his gnawing conscience seized him. But his mind refused to take hold of the tangled tale of Oedipus, his anger and self-inflicted blindness, and he began to shape the apology he would make to Mr. Sutton. Not that he would accept *his* offer of tuition to Ohio University, not that he was even sure he would want to attend Ohio University—but he would explain that he had made his plans for college, that he was waiting to hear from M (University of Michigan was Miss Tillotson's *alma mater*, her recommendation of the school he should attend), and H (Harvard was Mr. Spiker's recommendation of the school he should attend). Mr. Spiker had often remarked that it was his expectation that one of his students would someday attend Harvard, and he had come to Lighthorse in October with a thick crimson catalogue in one hand and its mailing wrapper in the other, saying, "This just came in the morning mail. You're our Harvard candidate if ever we're to have one, Lighthorse." He laid an arm on Lighthorse's shoulder. "And we're going to get you a full tuition scholarship unless my judgment is far enough off base to be thrown out by a catcher with a wooden arm."

In November Lighthorse had applied to Harvard and Michigan, along with Ohio State University as backup, although it had been his inclination to apply to smaller colleges closer home, perhaps Muskingum or Kent State. As for Ohio University, he hadn't even read its catalogue, but he remembered that Mr. Spiker had mentioned it was his *alma mater* and he considered it a good college "much like Ohio State, but smaller." Who would have supposed that Mr. Spiker and Mr. Sutton had attended the same college? Or that Nancy Sutton would decide to attend Ohio University?

Had he known—Lighthorse was underlining "What

about OU?" on the calendar before him—he could just as well have applied to Ohio University as his backup college, rather than Ohio State. Lighthorse reread his calendar entry, closed Sophocles' THREE PLAYS, turned off the desk lamp, closed and locked the door to The Stall. He went directly to his locker for his jacket, and on his way out of the building stopped in Mr. Spiker's office to pick up the green-and-white catalogue labeled "Ohio University."

It was Friday afternoon before Lighthorse completed his application to Ohio University. He recorded his action on the desk calendar: "Still owe Mr. Sutton A. Seize the day!" With his mind at peace he carried the Ohio University application toward the post office, thinking he would stop by the bank *after* he had mailed the bulky letter. But his plans were abruptly changed in the post office, for as he slipped the Ohio University letter into the outgoing mail slot, Adrienne Whatman, the mail clerk, handed him a letter that bore the return address of The Admissions Office, University of Michigan, Ann Arbor, Michigan. Because he had been concentrating on Ohio University's green-and-white—green leaves, white blossoms and Nancy's face—he accepted the letter in dark blue lettering without much thought as to what it might be.

Stepping out the door and under the overcast sky he tore open the envelope and read: "Dear Harry: We regret to inform you. . ." Slowly he read the letter through a second time, his eyes blurring. The calculated gentle phrasing sank home, phrasing that explained there was the stiffest competition nationwide for the limited number of scholarships and class spaces set aside at the University of Michigan for out-of-state students, and that they were extremely sorry he would not be one of that number.

Refolding the letter along its original creases he shoved

it back into its envelope. As much as the letter stung him, it would be an even more bitter pill for Miss Tillotson—he would have to find some way to let her know, but gently, kindly. Lighthorse glanced around—the sky seemed to have grown dark and ominous during his moments in the post office—and discovered himself in front of the Moravian Church. Concentrating on the letter in his hand he had walked right past the bank and had crossed the street and was well on his way back to the high school. Now, rather than go back to apologize to Mr. Sutton at the bank as he had planned, he continued at a jog to the school and through the shadowy hall that still smelled faintly of the vegetable soup served to the bussed students at noontime. At least he had arrived during the last class period and need encounter no one in the halls. He mounted the stairs two at a time and headed for the sanctuary of The Stall.

His eyes were adjusting to the shadows, and as he bent to fit the key into the lock, he noticed a piece of paper tucked beneath the door. The door in opening swept the paper across the floor. He turned on the lamp and knelt to pick up the folded sheet of lined notebook paper on which was printed: "Urgent."

"Now what?" he murmured as he unfolded the sheet and read: "Lighthorse, whoa!" (The handwriting shouted a name that set his blood racing.)

As sure as my middle name is the same as yours, and as much as I've always wanted my last name to match my middle, I hope you will read this all the way through before throwing it away. I must see you tonight. I must, I must!

If ever I had need of a brother, it's now. Daddy went by train to a bank meeting in Cleveland. He collapsed and is in the Cleveland Clinic, and I've got to drive there. Will you go with me? Come after supper, as soon as possible.

Nance (her X)

I told Ted Biggers I was going to write this to you (I didn't ask Hitler, Mussolini, or him, and never will) and he told me you'd thumb your nose at me. Please don't.

❧ 27 ❧

At 8:00 p.m. on Friday, February 19, 1938, Lighthorse sat behind the wheel of Mr. Sutton's Buick coupe, which bore Nancy and him through the wintry night toward Cleveland. The macadam road unwound ahead, a dark path increasingly clotted with white as the snowfall continued, heavy and persistent. Wavering between disbelief and wonderment, Lighthorse let his hand fall from the steering wheel to the pocket of Nancy's two hands waiting, and touched for an instant the fine flesh of her wrist. While he fought to control the hunger in his hands, he thought: "He takes with one hand, gives with the other."

"I heard that," Nancy murmured. "What did you say?"

"Nothing. Nothing."

"You mumbled something."

"Nothing," Lighthorse said. He allowed his forefinger to caress her wrist. "No plans, nothing."

"Who can plan anything when something like this occurs?" Nancy said. "Daddy's illness, his operation, this snowstorm. One has as much chance for independent action or free will as one of these snowflakes."

Lighthorse thought of Gerard Manley Hopkins, his theory that divine essence distinguishes every single thing, so why not suppose that each snowflake knows who it is, where it comes from, where it belongs. He said: "Things work out, Nance. Your father will be all right. After all, the Cleveland Clinic's not the morgue." He heard her indrawn breath and added: "Forgive me. I didn't mean to use that word."

"That's all right. The whole world's just one giant morgue anyhow." Her voice broke.

"Nance—Nance!" Lighthorse drew her against him. Her anguish and her beauty wrenched him. She pulled away but not before he caught the glint of moisture in her eyes. "Nance, Nance," he whispered.

She drew a deep breath and said: "You would never know how hard I tried to make things up to Daddy, after—after last summer. He'd been getting on me about not studying, not using my mind, and I did my damnedest to do that."

"I saw it," Lighthorse said. "I saw it and Mr. Spiker saw it. He really admires you, Nance. Your mind, your spirit, your independence. He's mentioned it several times, and I'm sure he told your father."

"I wouldn't bank on what Mr. Spiker thinks of—" Nancy stopped. "Bad pun."

Lighthorse waited. He wondered if he ought to ask in detail about her father, but decided not to. Finally he said, "Would you care to hear a little song?"

Nancy was incredulous. "Oh sure, that's exactly what I need now—a merry, merry little song. Lighthorse, sometimes. . ."

"I didn't mean that kind of song. I had in mind something

more personal." Again Lighthorse waited, and in the silence became aware of the crunch of the wheels on the carpet of snow and the steady slip-slap of the windshield wiper. Then he sang: "I will care for you/ So long as there's a sky above/ I'll walk free throughout the world/ Nourished by faith and love/ So long as a field is green/ I will treasure you/ For you taught me to cherish/ What is beautiful and true." He hummed the tune and then sang the words a second time.

Nancy glanced at him, smiled, and said quietly: "Redundant as a snowstorm, isn't it?"

"Sure, but most songs are redundant—and emotions too. That's why they last. Anyway, that's our song. I wrote it for you this past weekend—when I was thinking I might never get to speak to you again. I thought I might just slip it into your locker or leave it on your desk. Hey, what gives? You're laughing *and* crying." He craned his neck to look out the window. "There must be a rainbow somewhere."

"It's—it's just like you, Lighthorse. That song, your comment, oh you guy!" She leaned forward to brush her lips to his and he felt her tears dampen his cheek. "I love the song, Lighthorse." She pulled free of his encircling arm and felt in her purse for a handkerchief. After a moment she said, "Isn't the road getting awfully slippery?"

"A trifle."

"We could stop if we had to—if you thought we should. Daddy would want us to. He wouldn't want us to risk our lives getting to him just because he's in the hospital."

"You said they already operated?"

"At nine this morning. I—I didn't even know they were thinking of operating. He was sick with a stomach ulcer last fall, then he seemed to get that under control. He was in such good health we drove to Sanibel Island for the holidays, then something happened a couple weeks ago. All of a sudden he got very sick again—vomiting and passing blood —and now this." Nancy had turned her head, and Lighthorse, sensing her eyes on him, leaned forward to adjust the heater.

"Well?" she asked.

"Nancy," Lighthorse said, "you know—did you know your father came to talk with me about college? Did you know that?"

"He told me he'd gone to speak to Mr. Spiker, and that Mr. Spiker had showed him The Stall. He said he couldn't believe you were reading all the books in that room."

"He—your father—didn't mention any particulars?" The car slipped sideways; Lighthorse spun the wheel in time to counter the skid.

Nancy said nothing. They were passing through a crossroads town named "Tuscarawas." How blind we are, even in what appear moments of prescience, Lighthorse thought. He wondered if he should tell her he had been rejected by Michigan.

"Don't you suppose we should stop?" Nancy asked. "We'll be in New Philadelphia shortly. We could get a room there if need be."

"I hope the roads will be clearer there. We'll see."

They passed through New Philadelphia and Dover, and decided to go on, though the roads were no clearer. They drove through the blustering night into what had become by now a white bowl lined with snow, impenetrable ten feet ahead of their headlights, and yet to Lighthorse it seemed idiotic to wonder what lay beyond the walls of snow. Their actual stop—when it occurred—surprised them both into exclamations of amazement.

They had passed one after another of the little towns beyond Dover, and a corporation sign, illegible in the snow but identifiable by its standard shape and its relationship to the shadowy outlines of several houses, had just announced a new town when suddenly the road slid sharply downhill to the right. The front wheels turned to follow the road, but the car kept going straight ahead. So fast they moved, the car felt stationary and the road seemed to be gliding, and suddenly they were stationary, still upright, in a drift well off the road.

Lighthorse opened his door; the night was a white whirl. The snow was running-board deep, and somewhat packed where the car had slid across it, but the drift didn't appear one that would hold them. He put the car in reverse, the wheels spun but the drift held. He tried rocking the car backward and forward, this at the direction of Nancy, who had stepped out into the shallower snow on the road. He shifted gears and rocked the car backward and forward but still the drift held. Finally he got out and said: "The damned drift isn't that deep. Why don't you drive, and I'll push."

The drift continued to hold when Nancy got in to drive and he strained against the back bumper. He ran wide to the front of the car and pushed from there; the wheels spun as Nancy gunned the motor again and again but the drift held. Finally when the air was heavy with blue smoke and gas fumes, Nancy turned off the key.

"Well, Lighthorse old pal, old partner, we're parked, or might as well be. I guess we'll call this home. Now"— her voice mixed anxiety and joy—"now we can just be ourselves and let Daddy wait."

"Yes, due to my driving, we'll make a cozy little stop in this town. I wonder what and where this town is—and if they have a garage with a tow-truck?" Lighthorse sighted the surrounding dark with a hand over his eyes, settling finally upon the single row of houses that lined the right side of the street. "Didn't I see a corporation sign at the top of the last grade? You wait here while I take a look."

"I don't think you need do that. If there is a town it's up ahead; we might just as well walk there now."

"You're right, absolutely right." Lighthorse leaned close, put his arm around her, and said, "I'll tell you a secret: I'm feeling lightheaded. Maybe just being with you—"

"So am I." She coughed. "I think it's the exhaust fumes —but at least we've got this headache together." She leaned against him.

Lighthorse laughed and said: "I shouldn't have used that word 'secret'—but when I tell *you* things it's like thinking or telling them to myself."

"I always wanted you to tell me things; I wanted to share everything, everything."

"My brother Elmo told me how to keep a secret. I think he got his notion from Emerson. Do you know Emerson's 'Sphinx'?"

"No, but I'm listening."

Lighthorse spoke slowly: "Here's the last stanza: 'Through a thousand voices/ spoke the universal dame/ who telleth one of my meanings/ is master of all I am.'"

At the word "master" Nancy bridled. "How horrible! You don't—can't believe that, Lighthorse."

"Not entirely but in part. Everything always seems a part of something else. Knowing a part I can usually make a guess at the rest." He looked down and found her dark eyes charged with a fierce light. He laughed. "Knowing I fouled up and stuck us in this snowdrift I can guess we're going to walk." He reached in and flicked off the Buick's headlights.

"But to be master—to know everything. Lighthorse, that would be terrible."

"Why would it?" Lighthorse asked. He wasn't sure what

she meant, where her comment was headed, but he sensed he had blundered.

"Knowing what we have to know is too much, the load is just too much, too heavy to carry," Nancy said. She waited beside him while he locked the car.

Lighthorse reached an arm around her as they picked their way across the road to the narrow sidewalk, and followed it. They walked for five minutes or so—the road turned sharply to the right again—and they came to a Sohio Filling Station. It was dark except for a lighted clock that was not running. Beyond the filling station they came to a red brick building optimistically named "City Hall." It was lighted by a bare bulb extending from the end of a crooked pipe that reminded Lighthorse of a kiln fireman's poker. Lighthorse tried the blackened door of the "City Hall" but it was locked, and so they went on to two stores and their clear, cold, lighted-from-within plate glass windows. Ahead they could see only unbroken darkness, except for the dim glow from widely separated street lights; and the street lights themselves ended some three blocks ahead. They stopped and were about to return to the car when a door opened some four houses down the street. Whoever opened the door did so only to close it firmly, for the door banged shut but not before they saw the small sign "Rooms—By the day or week."

"I wonder about one night," Nancy said.

The building they moved toward was square, a large box of three stories, boasting a few remnants of white paint and slightly more of green trim. Several of its square windows showed lights behind drawn shades, and they could now see a sign above the door: "Newton Inn."

"Having surveyed the town we chose to stay at the Newton!"

"Me and my stupid driving," Lighthorse said.

"Come in, sweet fig." Nancy laughed. "Enter the Newton and forget the past."

Lighthorse pushed against the narrow door; it swung wide, scraping the linoleum-covered floor in the little hallway that opened into a cavernous lobby, dimly lighted by three green-shaded bulbs. To the right of the lobby, fenced off by oak paneling, was a smaller room containing a desk and an ancient green safe, its door ajar. Above the desk was a single bulb on a long cord. On the opposite side of the lobby sat four men, gathered near the only lamps in the room. Two were playing cards, one was writing in a small account book, the fourth was reading a paper.

Lighthorse walked to what he took to be the office, stuck his head through the aperture, and asked, "Clerk?"

"That's Burt, he's out." The man wearing horn-rimmed glasses spoke without raising his eyes from the printed page.

"Is he expected back soon?"

"Not tonight," the man in the horn-rims replied, still reading.

"Well, we wanted to get a room—two rooms."

"Just help yourself. The keys are hanging there on the board and the little paddle gives you the number." The horn-rimmed reader folded his paper and looked toward Lighthorse. Then he caught sight of Nancy who had unbuttoned her coat and was shaking snow from her hair. With widening eyes the man in the glasses swept her head to toe, his lips rounding over his indrawn whistle.

Lighthorse glanced at Nancy and saw the blaze of dark beauty that had rocked the man in horn-rims. He ignored him. "How much will the rooms be? We'd like two rooms with baths—at least one that way."

"Nope. You can't have 'em." The man continued staring at Nancy. "You'll just take your bath at the end of the hall or not at all. They're two dollars fifty each—the rooms, that is."

"I'll sign the register," Lighthorse said, pulling an ink-stained ledger toward him. "Here Nancy," he whispered, "you'd better sign too."

"It don't matter whether you sign or not," the horn-rimmed man said. Then he chuckled. "If I was you two I'd take one room anyhow."

At this comment, one of the card players looked up. He echoed the laughter and nudged the second player and the three of them sat staring at Nancy as if struck by lightning.

Lighthorse lowered his voice. "Do you want to wait here while I get the luggage?"

"I'll come too."

On the way back to the car, Lighthorse said, "You aren't afraid?"

"Afraid, with you?" Her hand was on his arm and they went skating along. "I would sort of like to be in the same room with you, though."

"Maybe we'll find one with two beds. Do you think I should ask?"

"I wouldn't."

"I'll have to ask about paying."

"It's all right to ask that."

When they came back to the hotel, Lighthorse asked the horn-rimmed reader, "Could you tell me about paying—should I pay in advance?"

"Not unless you have a mind to." The man laughed to himself, as if he had come unexpectedly upon a joke on the sporting page. "Mister," he said as Lighthorse moved off, "if there's no one on duty in the morning, you just leave your keys and your money beside the register. Burt'll find them."

"I've never seen a hotel like this one," Nancy said as they got out of hearing on the carpeted stairs.

"You probably have to look quick or it'll be gone—in the snow and dark."

"But how does it stay in business?"

"Just be glad it has."

They took turns using the small rest room at the end of the hall before Lighthorse opened the door to room number fifteen. By the hall light he was able to see the interior of the room: a bureau, a chair, a desk, and one double bed. "Only one bed. I'll try fourteen." He stepped across the hall and had some trouble unlocking the door. Finally he got the door open and Nancy said, "One bed. They're forcing us to it."

Lighthorse said, "Don't you think I should go and ask Horn-rim if there are any with two beds?"

"No," Nancy said. "One bed's all right with me—if you can stand a bed-fellow."

"A fellow!" Lighthorse exclaimed. He set the luggage in room fifteen and turned on the light. He went to the window that looked out on the street and raised the shade and then lowered it quickly. "Maybe I'd better wait."

"I don't think it matters. Only two voyeurs were out tonight, and they're both in this room." Nancy sat down on the bed, pulled off her fur-trimmed galoshes and kicked off her flat-heeled shoes. Lighthorse watched her a minute, reached out and patted her head and then went around the bed and sat down to remove his shoes. He began to unbutton his shirt, hesitated, and looked over his shoulder. Her arms flashed above her head as she took off her dress. He stopped unbuttoning his shirt and said, "Would you want me to leave the room?"

"Do I look that bad?" Nancy was smiling. "Maybe I'm

not the fastest undresser you've ever met, but do you really think speed's that important?"

Lighthorse reached across the bed and pulled her against him. His hands, rough from the cold, snagged her slip.

"That comes off too," she said, shaking him off and kneeling before her opened suitcase. "I've got a pair of pajamas someplace," she said. "I did have, I mean." She was rummaging beneath sweaters and blouses and now she looked up at Lighthorse.

"I've got a pair," Lighthorse said. He went to what had been Elmo's laundry mailing case and drew forth a pair of blue pajamas—the only pair of pajamas he had ever owned, those, a hunting jacket, two shirts, and three pairs of socks being his share of Elmo's wardrobe. "These will fit you with tuck-ins to spare," he said, holding out the pajamas.

"I could sleep in my slip. I've done it before."

"It'll be too cold! Here, take these."

"No. I may lead you way off to a stupid hotel, but I'm not going to steal your pajamas."

"Who's stealing? I'm giving them to you. Besides they're not really mine. I just inherited them."

"Okay, I'll make a deal. I'll wear the tops and you wear the bottoms. How's that for a bargain?"

"Suits me," Lighthorse said. "You get all set." He stepped around the chair over which he had hung his trousers, and facing away from Nancy lifted his share of the pajamas above his head and thrust his arms where the legs were to go.

"You clown—you've got the bottoms."

"Oh sure, now that you mention it." He swung both legs into the pajamas and collapsed into the chair in laughter. "You got yours on?"

175

"Ours! Sure, I'm practically in bed." She dove under the covers.

Lighthorse went to open the window. "This is pretty cozy —and private. You like fresh air?"

"Love it."

"Do you mind if I turn the light off?"

"Not at all. If you turn the light out, you can raise the shade and we'll be able to watch the snow falling."

Lighthorse raised the shade. "The snow must be letting up. I can see a street light."

"Good. I—I wanted to talk a little—ask you something."

"Such as?"

"Oh Lighthorse, I just wish you'd make love to me and let me listen."

"Nance, I can't. You told me you needed a brother and you've been trying to tell or ask me something since the moment you wrote that note. Is it something about your father—his operation?"

Nancy looked at him and shook her head.

"Well, your father's car is in the ditch, thanks to my asinine driving. I sure hope he can forget and forgive."

"Forget the car, just forget it, for god's sake."

Lighthorse pulled her against him. "Nance, were you trying to tell me something about your father and me— something beyond naming that I did?"

There was a long silence, and Nancy finally whispered, "I—I just can't—I just can't . . . understand."

"Well, if you won't tell me, I'll tell you." Lighthorse stumbled through his memory seeking words. "It's not right that you punish yourself, especially since I caused the whole thing. I mean it was bad enough the way I spoke to your father in Pittsburgh when I found out about Elmo's death. Then two weeks ago when he came to the school I really told him off. I really did. My god, I didn't mean what I said to sound the way it did, Nance, but words uttered are like blows struck. Mine in The Stall were cowardly, deadly."

Nancy sat bolt upright. "Look at me, Lighthorse, for I've got to tell you. It wasn't Daddy's idea that he come to you and offer to pay your tuition at Ohio University. That was my idea. And do you really want to know why I made him come to you and make that offer? Do you know why I made him do that?"

"He said you were going to Ohio University—he said it was the school you wanted to attend."

"Lighthorse, Ted Biggers has been accepted at Ohio University, and he's going to enroll there. And I just happen to know . . ."

"For god's sake, Nancy, I'm not jealous of Ted Biggers— and never have been. Look, you're here with me and not with Ted Biggers. You didn't turn to him when you needed someone."

"Lighthorse, one minute more and I'm going to stuff this fist in your mouth." Nancy had shaped her hand into a fist.

"Boy, I think you mean that."

"You're damned right I mean it. Lighthorse, please listen to what I have to say: I happen to know because I've been told at least a dozen times, the only reason Ted Biggers is going to enroll at Ohio University is because I'm going there. And because I've wasted so damned much of my life in Gnadenhutten fighting off Ted Biggers I made Daddy go to you and offer to pay your tuition. Don't you see? Can't you understand?"

Lighthorse felt tears in his eyes, and knew he couldn't trust his voice. He was thankful for the shadows in the room as he stretched his arms and flexed his hands—momentarily he had felt they too might be beyond his control. He reached for Nancy and drew her to him. His lips touched her fingertips, her hair, her forehead, her cheeks as she wept—as they wept together.

Later he said, "He'll be all right, Nance. I'll wager my life on it, he'll be all right."

How long he held her and comforted her he could not say but finally she grew quiet in his arms. Still he held her until he felt her relax and breathe deeply, and when she was sound asleep he lowered her to the pillow, pulled the covers about her neck, and stretched out beside her. He longed for sleep, but could not find it. He turned to face the window and found himself drawn to it. He stared out on snowy waste grown visible: street, a dark huddle of houses and light poles and trees, and a distant ridge of hills.

Cold claimed his feet and legs, his hands and arms, his ears and nose, and still he stared into the night. That which he was, whatever he was, he felt roll back into a smaller and smaller ball. At last he sensed himself at one with street, trees, and distant hills, as cold and dull and distant; he rocked on deadened feet, shivered, and went to sit on the bed. He heard Nancy turn toward him but he sat with his face in his hands, and was sitting so as the morning sun crept in to warm the frigid air.

≫ 28 ≪

Nancy was not awake when he got up from the bed and lowered the window. He gathered his clothes and made his way down the hall to the bathroom where he got a drink from his cupped hands, lighted the antique gas heater, bathed and shaved, and got a second drink. He returned to the room, put on his shoes and jacket and went downstairs. He met no one in the hall or in the lobby which still reeked of cigar smoke, but in the street he was pleasantly surprised to find a mechanic unlocking the door to the filling station they had found deserted the night before. The mechanic climbed into his red tow truck, invited Lighthorse onto the seat beside him, apologizing for the chains and block-and-tackle which forced Lighthorse to hold his knees at eye height as they roared along the snow-clogged street.

Once the Buick was on the road and Lighthorse had paid the three-dollar charge, the mechanic pushed his greasy cap back from his thick red hair and said, "Buddy, you can be damned glad you slid down this bank last night and not last year."

"How's that?" Lighthorse asked.

"Last year this was a ravine—just one big ravine. The Highway Department hauled fill for a couple weeks to level it. I guess there's always something to be thankful for."

"Sure," Lighthorse said. "There always is."

"Two weeks can make a helluva difference in a hole when the Highway Department starts running those yellow graders up and down."

"You are so right." Lighthorse nodded and the driver returned to his cab. Lighthorse sat gunning the Buick motor. The tow truck started forward, and the wheels of the Buick took hold and he slowly made his way, following the tow truck's tracks, to the oversized salt box labeled "Newton Inn."

When he opened the door of the room he found Nancy fully dressed, tossing the covers back, carefully remaking the bed. "Hey, look who's already up!" he said.

"Hair combed, lipstick on—I knew you'd want to get started."

Lighthorse sensed that he was hearing a rehearsed response. "Aren't you even thirsty? I was."

"I got a drink down the hall. Thanks anyway."

He took hold of the coverlet and flipped it across the bed. "I got the car back on the road; a mechanic at that garage down the street was just opening up and went right out."

"Wonderful!" She pulled the coverlet into place over the pillow. "Oops! Just a minute." She reached under the pillow she had used. "Here are your pajamas—my half of them."

Lighthorse took them and stuffed them into the laundry mailing case. "They really belonged to Elmo. He bought them and he'd sure turn a handspring—"

"Did he dislike me that much?"

Lighthorse concentrated on tightening the straps on the

laundry case. "He hardly knew you. He did think you might keep me from going to college. If you and I—oh, you know."

"Well, I guess he can rest in peace on that score. He still might resent the use of his pajamas, however." Nancy's voice was carefully modulated. "And I apologize for that display last night."

"Nance." Lighthorse moved toward her.

She avoided him. "I mean it. I woke up in the night and lay there in bed hating myself all the time you stood at the window and just sat there on the bed."

"Oh my god, you weren't awake!"

"Weren't you? And you were freezing too."

"I was just . . . half way thinking—and I never get cold when I'm in that state. I often ramble around at night thinking that way."

"*That way?* Lighthorse, you're not a good liar."

Nancy picked up her overnight bag and would have carried it to the car had Lighthorse not caught up with her. At the deserted desk he laid out the worn wooden paddles with keys attached, and counted out five dollars. "Maybe I should add a tip?"

"What for, room service?" Nancy picked up three of his dollars and placed a fifty-cent piece beside the remaining two. "We used only one room; we'll pay for only one room."

When they were in the car picking their way slowly out of town but going as fast as the roads permitted, she said, "I have to tell you about the dream I had."

"Last night?"

"When you were down the hall this morning. I'd been lying awake too and then I dozed off and before I knew it I was back home in my own bedroom—in Gnadenhutten, and Mother walked through the door wearing *my pajamas.*"

"Elmo's tops, you mean. That's understandable." Lighthorse laughed, for he felt the self-hatred in her tone and feared and dreaded it.

"No, in *my pajamas,* a pair of candy-striped pajamas Daddy gave me for my birthday when I was twelve. Anyhow, Mother came in wearing my pajamas—they seemed big enough and all—and she came over to where I was lying and pushed me over and got into bed beside me. Then the oddest thing happened. She was in bed beside me but not touching me, and I reached out my hand to touch her but—you won't believe this—my hand disappeared, fingers . . . palm . . . wrist. I could feel and even see them and then they were gone, and my arm, and in a minute my legs and stomach and chest and head—then I was completely gone. Just gone. It was horrible. And the worst part was I knew she was still lying there."

"That is an odd one. I'd have thought you'd have wakened just as you disappeared—to find yourself here." Lighthorse reached toward her, but she drew back.

"That wasn't all. While I was gone, but knew Mother was lying there in my bed, you came walking through the doorway."

"That's one doorway I've not walked through."

"You came walking through the doorway and I tried desperately to stop you, for you were going right toward my bed and I just knew you were going to get into bed *with her.*"

"Did I?"

"I don't know—that's when I woke up."

"What was I wearing? Was I wearing something of your father's?"

"No. You were wearing Elmo's pajamas, the bottoms just as you wore them last night. But in the dream you weren't any six feet tall. Oh, you were at the beginning—when you stood in the doorway."

"Big as life and twice as natural, eh?"

"Don't laugh, please."

"I'm not, Nance . . . oh Nance!"

She went on: "You were natural enough to make me want you but you got smaller and smaller as you went toward the bed—and it seemed a long walk."

"I didn't disappear?"

"Not till I woke up. It was horrible, just horrible."

Lighthorse said: "But you woke up and you're here now."

"Yes, now. But the worst part of it all was that I don't know what happened. It's terrible to feel yourself disappear and not even know if it helped someone you love."

Lighthorse wanted to find a light phrase but couldn't. "I think you help someone by sticking around—someone you love, I mean."

"I wish you'd told Daddy that last week." Nancy paused. "Even in the dream I didn't really want to disappear but I did—or got replaced by Mother."

"You'll never get replaced, Nance." Lighthorse put his arm around her. "Let's see your tongue." She hesitated, then thrust the tip of her tongue between her gleaming teeth. He said: "Just as I thought—Pink Tongue!"

≫ 29 ≪

In the hall of the Cleveland Clinic they waited. Beneath the half door they could see the white-stockinged legs of the nurses moving here and there, and when they spoke it was only in hushed tones as though they dared not trust themselves to speak. "Maybe I should go first," Nancy said. "That way he'll be forewarned."

"Do. If he's able to see me, tell him I'm here, that I wanted to come, but give him a chance to refuse to see me."

"He won't do that—I wish you'd forget that idea."

"Here they come." Lighthorse motioned.

"You can come in now," announced the older of the two nurses.

"I'll just wait here," Lighthorse explained, seating himself again in one of the three wicker chairs in the hall. He looked away to avoid conversation, hoping to hear the talk within the room. Other than a soft exchange of greeting, he heard only a dozen mumbled sentences and then Nancy was beckoning him. He entered the room behind her and

184

found himself looking into a face he scarcely recognized, a face that had registered a history of pain since last they met.

"Mr. Sutton," Lighthorse said, laying his hand on the hand that rested outside the sheet.

"Lighthorse—you rascal."

"I wanted to come. Nancy told me she was coming so I just tagged along."

"Good." Mr. Sutton worked his lips into a smile. A little later he asked, "You drove up this morning? You made good time."

Lighthorse saw that Nancy had been so intent upon forestalling complex questions she was unprepared for the obvious. "We came right along, thanks to your Buick," he said.

"I'm glad you did the driving, Lighthorse."

"Oh he's a careful driver. And he and I have talked over a good many things." Nancy's eyes rested on Lighthorse. "He was coming here all primed with apologies and such, but I told him he should know you better than that."

"Good girl."

"I can speak for myself," Lighthorse said. "I'm glad you let me come, Mr. Sutton." He stopped and got a better hold on his voice. "I sort of wanted to explain about colleges. . . ."

Mr. Sutton protested with upthrust finger but Lighthorse went on: "I had meant to come to speak to you at the bank but then I got Nancy's invitation so I can tell you right here."

"Right," Mr. Sutton said.

"I had applied to Harvard and Michigan and Ohio State," Lighthorse said. "I was feeling pretty smug about it. No, not really, but I hadn't even considered Ohio University. When you spoke of it I knew how stupid I had been if Nancy was going there. Anyway, I've already heard from Michigan and they've turned me down. And if Michigan turned me down then I'd guess my chances at Harvard are just about nil. That leaves Ohio State—and since it has to admit me, I'll probably get in there." Lighthorse paused.

"What about Ohio State?" Mr. Sutton asked Nancy, but she nodded to Lighthorse, who said, "After you spoke of Ohio University—once I knew Nancy was going there, I got on the ball and made an application. Mailed it yesterday afternoon, in fact."

"Good for you." Mr. Sutton smiled. "Now if I just get on my feet and get ready to pay a couple hundred tuitions—" The corners of his eyes were crinkling.

"I won't go if I don't get a scholarship," Lighthorse said. He turned to include Nancy: "It's suddenly more important to me that I get a scholarship to Ohio University than to Harvard, if you know what I mean?"

Mr. Sutton said, "I've been lying here dreaming and thinking, thinking all sorts of crazy things. Now some of them begin to make sense."

"Bankers aren't supposed to think. They count. I know one who really counts." Nancy leaned over to hug her father.

"Count me in, not out. And no balanced balance sheet or column of figures at a time like this. This banker would trade a vault for an ice-cream cone and a boy's stomach to eat it with."

"You mean you've been lying here thinking that?"

"Exactly that—and more. Believe it or not, I've been worrying about you, Nancy."

Nancy glanced at Lighthorse; her lips parted but no words came, as if she didn't trust herself to speak.

"I was worried for fear that Ted Biggers would walk off with Nancy." Mr. Sutton directed his words to Lighthorse.

"I was so worried I did my damndest to ride herd on her until you got back your 20–20 vision, Lighthorse."

"Oh please!" Nancy exclaimed. "Do you have to make me sound like a—a cow?"

"The proper word is heifer, dear," Mr. Sutton said, "and most people know the difference."

Lighthorse felt the blood at his temples, felt his scar throbbing. "I've never been exactly blind," he managed to say. "And now that I've got back my 20–20 vision, I'll keep both eyes on her from now on. You can count on that."

"Good. That counting I will do—and count my erratic pulse and these ceiling tiles with a happier mind." A moment later Mr. Sutton murmured, "I too would like to be wrapped round by loving arms when the great moment comes."

"Daddy, you. . ."

"Of course not! Just wait till Dr. Kettering gives you his report. He's positively enthusiastic—despite this faded rose of a complexion." To Lighthorse he added, "They'll have the report on the tissue in a few days and then I'll be sure. I'm feeling better by the instant."

Lighthorse said, "Now I know I'm welcome."

"Welcome? You've just come home, son. And the wonderful part is here in this room—now—you two! This is exactly what I've always wanted."

Later, as they walked to the car, Nancy pulled Lighthorse close. "It was nice of you to say that about keeping your eyes on me—to say that to him at this time."

"It was easy, it's the truth." Lighthorse held her at arm's length. "Speaking truth, I'm a bit dazzled at how light I feel."

"I feel Lighthorse light myself," Nancy said as she escaped and ran toward the car.

187

⊰ 30 ⊱

During their long afternoon drive snow fell intermittently from a roily sky: it screened the familiar streets and houses of Gnadenhutten, and permitted them to arrive at the Sutton home as if it were the only house in town.

"Out of space, out of time," Lighthorse remarked as the filmy curtain enclosed them on the porch and Nancy fished the key from her purse to unlock the front door. "I always regarded this house that way," he explained, "out of space, out of time. I felt that my first night here. Do you remember?"

Nancy flipped the melting snow from her piled hair, exclaiming, "When Mother felt good about it she called it her house of myth. So enter the house of myth." She stepped through the doorway and Lighthorse followed, turning on the lights. He went from room to room adjusting the hot water heaters.

"Make it like it was on our first night, make it that way again," Nancy called after him. She removed her galoshes and her coat, then draped her coat over her shoulders and sat down at the piano.

Smetana's *Moldau* flowed forth to Lighthorse as he lighted the fire that had been laid in the fireplace, and the happy sadness of the music washed the immediate past from his mind.

"What does it say to you?" he asked, coming back to Nancy.

"Too much. Everything."

"As a river—our river?"

"It says give me intensity and depth, and let duration go hang." Nancy shook off her coat and kept playing, moving her head to the music. "Or even better—it says: Deep is the deep the great fish keep. Listen."

Lighthorse listened, nodding.

"Don't you love that?" Nancy said. "That was the first thing of her own that Mother taught me, part of a prayer from her Cherokee grandmother, the first thing she was taught."

"Deep is the deep the great fish keep," Lighthorse repeated.

"Oh Lighthorse—we're not—we're not apart, not pried apart?"

Lighthorse laughed and stooped to kiss her neck.

"We're not?" Nancy kept on with her playing.

Lighthorse lifted her coat and hung it in the closet. "Can our river be made to stop flowing when it is a river because it flows." He returned to touch his lips to her hair and ears and neck. He caressed her back and then stepped to the window looking out upon the side lawn. The snow had stopped falling and the moon shone through the clouds, laying blue shadows of apple trees across the whiter blanket that hid the grass. *Moldau* accompanied him. He watched two rabbits hop over the bank from the lawn next. They came to an apple tree and bounced around and around it. Finally one stopped and dug into the snow, rolled an apple free, and the other came and they set to work on it. Lighthorse turned to summon Nancy; she was beside him, watching.

"They and their apples, you and your turnips! That was such a wonderful time, Lighthorse." Nancy paused, then added, "You were sweet to do as you did last night, Lighthorse."

He walked her toward the fire. *Moldau* still accompanied him, in his mind.

She turned out the lights and they settled in front of the fireplace where the larger apple logs were beginning to kindle. Firelight met moonlight where they settled. They talked of their parents, two missionaries, two Indian myths, ninety Indian martyrs, Sled Hill, and the town. They talked of colleges, Harvard and Radcliffe maybe, Ohio University surely. As they talked the logs before them consumed themselves, filling the room with their substance transpired.

A log fell from the andirons in a scarlet shower and Lighthorse said:

> "*. . . and blue-bleak embers, ah my dear,*
> *Fall, gall themselves, and gash gold-vermillion.*"

"Appleness from applewood," Nancy whispered as she raised his hand to her lips.